Tales From Paradise
June Knox-Mawer

June Knox-Mawer is W............................broadcaster.
During the 1950s she live............A............................to the
Pacific, where her husban.................................books include
The Sultans Came to Tea, A .... Islands, A South Sea Spell
and *Marama of the Islands,* and she is a frequent broadcaster
on BBC Radio 4.

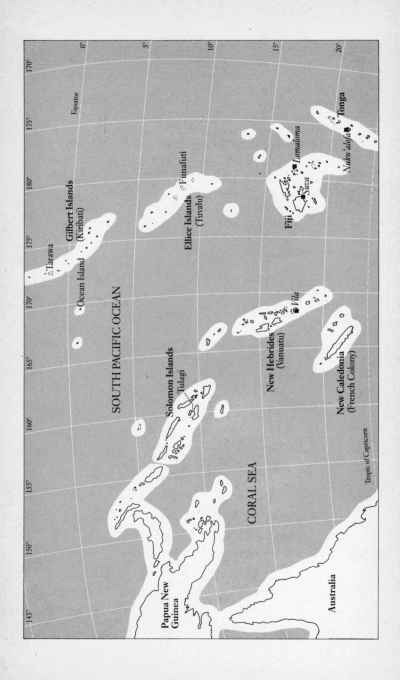

TALES FROM PARADISE

MEMORIES OF THE BRITISH
· IN THE SOUTH PACIFIC ·

June Knox-Mawer

ARIEL BOOKS
BBC PUBLICATIONS

A six-part series entitled 'Tales from Paradise', presented by June Knox-Mawer and produced by Julian Hale, was first broadcast on BBC Radio 4 in 1986.

Cover (inset) photograph shows Sir Ronald Garvey, as Governor of Fiji, being carried ashore with Lady Garvey in traditional South Sea style.

Map by Line and Line.

Published by BBC Publications
a division of BBC Enterprises Ltd
35 Marylebone High Street, London WIM 4AA

First published 1986

ISBN 0 563 20460 5

Typeset in 10 on 11pt Ehrhardt
by Phoenix Photosetting, Chatham
Printed in Great Britain by Mackays of Chatham Ltd

Contents

Acknowledgements

'Tales from Paradise' was given its original blessing as a radio series by David Hatch, Controller Radio 4, and set in motion by Helen Fry, Chief Producer, Sound Archive Features, whose insight and encouragement I have valued for many years. Chief architect of the series has been Julian Hale. Working with him to create a final shape out of a hundred hours of tape was a totally rewarding experience which has left me with the greatest admiration for his gifts as a producer. My gratitude is due to all three.

I would also like to put on record my special thanks to Stephen Shipley, who took on a large share of the touring and recording; to our secretary Melanie Grocott; to Donald Simpson and his staff at the library of the Royal Commonwealth Society; to Liz Mardell for her Fiji contributions; and to Philip Snow for his expert advice on many points of custom and language.

At BBC Publications I am indebted to Sheila Ableman who commissioned the book and to my brilliant editor Nina Shandloff; also to Jennifer Fry, who organised the picture research, and to Gillian Shaw for the design.

I would also like to thank Duckworth, the publishers, for permission to quote from *My South Sea Island* by Eric Muspratt.

The one vital ingredient, of course, was the co-operation of the contributors. Their patience and enthusiasm – and the island-style hospitality dispensed along the way – made work a pleasure. I only hope we have communicated something of that pleasure to our readers.

Introduction

It was March 1958 when I encountered my first South Sea island. I was on my way to Fiji where my husband was to be Chief Magistrate, and the green blur on the horizon was Pitcairn, last resting place of the *Bounty*. The isolation of that tiny outpost, and the sight of the descendants of the mutineers rowing out through the breakers to greet us, crystallised for me all the romance of the European connection with the Pacific.

Over the next twelve years I visited many a lonely island as I travelled about, trying to capture in my books the changing life of the people. Intertwined with the Polynesians, Melanesians and Micronesians was that other picturesque race – the British. They cropped up everywhere – not only the administrators who ran what were then colonial territories, but also teachers and missionaries, planters and traders, and the eccentric flotsam and jetsam of more adventurous times.

Long after leaving the islands, one wintry afternoon outside Broadcasting House in London, I met Charles Allen, whose series of 'Tales' from the Raj, the Dark Continent and the South China Seas I much admired. He suggested that I should add the Pacific to this archive of imperial memories. The BBC took up the idea, and the result was a six-part Radio 4 series 'Tales from Paradise' and this book, encompassing some forty interviews and more than half a century of experience.

In many ways this is a totally different story from the general run of colonial history. Cook's voyages and the Western image of the noble savage had created a special kind of relationship from the start. In Victorian times, in a reversal of the usual practice, Fiji finally persuaded the British to annex the islands as a possession of the Crown. The first Governor, Sir Arthur Gordon, made the point in no uncertain terms: 'It should always be remembered that this is emphatically not a white man's colony ... The Queen reigns here by virtue of a voluntary cession of rights to her by the native rulers and owners of these islands.' In areas such as the

Solomons, the British were expected not so much to administer as simply to 'keep the peace' – a legacy of the nineteenth-century efforts of the Royal Navy to preserve law and order between the tribes and the settlers.

Not surprisingly, this was no place for the autocratic splendours of the Raj or the vast complexities of the African system. For the most part the usual charge of colonial exploitation was equally hard to apply. Firm personal friendships have survived independence, and nostalgic reunions take place whenever a rugby tour or ministerial conference brings the islanders to Britain.

The various High Commissions keep up the official links in London. But most of the 'old hands' have gone to ground elsewhere. My interviewing circuit often took me to places such as Bognor and Bournemouth, where the sea is a reminder of the Pacific and a southern breeze is the next best thing to the familiar trade winds. Even now, the years spent in the islands still seem to dominate most other experiences. Arranged around those very English sitting-rooms are the mementoes to prove it – shell necklaces, shark's-teeth swords and wooden *kava* bowls embossed with a silver plaque commemorating the years of service. On the mantelpiece are faded sepia photographs of long-vanished chiefs and governors, garden parties under the palm trees, bungalows by a lagoon.

But more real somehow are the memories, those individual images of the past that the tape recorder can preserve for the future. They have been called 'Tales from Paradise' – bearing in mind that even paradise has its flaws, as well as the occasional serpent.

I

On Probation

'Going into the Colonial Service!' remonstrated an industrial tycoon of the 1920s to the young Ronald Garvey, who was to become one of the foremost British administrators in the Pacific. 'You'll be nothing but a gentleman pauper all your life!'

Nowhere in the field of Empire was the post of a government official particularly lucrative. But because of the limited scale of its responsibilities, the Pacific service was the least rewarding of all from a financial point of view, nor was there the attraction of the glamorous social life enjoyed in capitals such as Singapore, New Delhi or Nairobi. Its status as a career posting was correspondingly low, and more often than not, young Colonial Office recruits were sent to the Pacific either by accident or for reasons of administrative convenience. In 1925, Ronald Garvey was on the brink of a career in Africa – that is, until his interview.

The first thing I was asked was, 'Well, where would you like to go?'

I said, 'Nigeria.'

'Why Nigeria?'

'Well,' I said, 'you see, I think the pay . . .'

But he didn't let me finish the sentence. 'Ah yes, the pagans,' he said. 'A most interesting anthropological subject.'

I wasn't interested in the pagans at all. It was the best-paid cadet job in the whole of the Colonial Empire at that time and I was referring to the salary.

Anyway, he went on to say that he saw from my papers that I'd been studying the Pacific. 'We have, of course, a protectorate out there, the Solomon Islands Protectorate,' he said. 'You wouldn't perhaps think of going there, would you? It's a small place, but the frogs can float to the top of a small pond quite quickly, can't they?'

However, the South Seas also had its own unique appeal. At the end of the 1920s Andrew Armstrong was looking for wider horizons than England had to offer. As with so many recruits, his image of an adventurous life in the islands dated back to his schooldays.

> When I was eleven I read an article in the *Boy's Own Paper* about the South Seas. You know the kind of thing, tremendous waves and canoes, and warriors with spears and shields. I suppose it stayed in the back of my mind when I applied for the Colonial Service. I was interviewed by a man who said, 'Well, there are one or two vacancies in the Pacific. But I must tell you that the District Officer and his assistant have just been murdered on the island of Malaita. Would that make any difference?'
>
> So I said, 'Of course not, sir,' as if murder was the daily routine as far as I was concerned.
>
> I heard no more for many weeks, then suddenly a letter arrived, offering me a cadetship in the Gilbert and Ellice Islands. So I hurried off to look at the map to see where they were.

Apparently one test question was, 'What would you do if you were shipwrecked on a desert island?' Another interviewee, a friend of Ronald Garvey's, replied that if he had a gun he would shoot himself. He was not selected.

Philip Snow, who joined in 1938, found that certain attributes were considered proper for a District Officer-to-be.

> I got the strong impression that they were looking for people who wouldn't go crackers in the solitude that was obviously going to face them. They wanted to know what sort of action I'd take if the people were rebellious, or became difficult to deal with. Would I, for instance, burn down their villages? I promptly disabused them of any idea that I might do that! Then they were particularly keen to know whether I played any games. They obviously felt that games in principle were a good thing for an administrator to do, to provide him with a special contact with the people.

For all cadet probationers, the next step was a year's training course at Oxford or Cambridge. Here the curriculum gave a brisk taste of things to come, ranging from tropical forestry to first aid and hygiene, civil and criminal law, typing and surveying. Philip Snow was disconcerted to find that no one was able to teach Fijian, though an 'exceedingly unmilitary' ex-Indian Army colonel gave Hindi lessons which were to prove invaluable in a colony where over half the population were Indians.

Finally came the kitting-out. According to David Trench, who was to become Governor of Hong Kong, this could be a disappointing experience.

We had a £40 uniform allowance, which was a fair amount of money in those days. We wandered around all the shops which dealt in tropical gear. But most of their stuff was more suitable for film producers and stars doing Tarzan movies than it was for impecunious cadets.

Nick Waddell, later Sir Alexander Waddell, received more specific instructions as he and a couple of fellow cadets prepared themselves for duty in the Solomons.

We were told to go to a large outfitters, where they produced a suggested list for the well-dressed tropical gentleman which included some strange things. The solar topee, for instance, was lined with silver foil to protect you from any sun that may have got through the helmet. Then I remember being fitted out with shirts that buttoned on the shoulders and the waist to accommodate what as known as a spine pad, worn to ward off the sun's rays from your back. After the spine pad, there was a thing called a cholera belt to wrap round your tummy – I don't know whether by day or by night or both.

Ronald Garvey received some additional advice from a District Officer on leave. Since the rainfall in the Solomons was heavy and 'the natives by no means fully civilised', he would find an umbrella and a revolver 'comforting possessions'.

Travelling out via the Panama Canal, which became the most frequent route, meant six weeks of gracious living, shipboard style, before reaching Sydney or Auckland. It was then something of a come-down to make the last stage of the journey in one of the shabby little trading steamers that plied the south-west archipelagos. Cockroaches abounded in the cramped cabins, but the sunshine on deck, and the shimmering expanses of blue on blue across the huge unbroken horizons of the Pacific, more than compensated for any discomfort.

Ahead lay the thrill of finally sighting one's destination. Dick Horton, bound for the Solomons on the SS *Malaita*, remembers his first glimpse of the little island which was then the government headquarters.

The morning of arrival, I was on deck at dawn. At first it was difficult to pick out Tulagi. Then there it was, tucked away in the arms of the bigger island of Gela. It was a lovely little island, with the palm trees coming up out of the haze, the epitome of all the South Sea islands we'd ever seen in films, and so neat and green, as if someone had taken a mowing machine and gone round the edges. The coral reefs surrounding the approaches stood out against the white of the surf, and the ship was steering a fairly tortuous course. I said to one of the crew that the skipper must have a tricky job getting in to harbour.

He pointed to a picturesque line of jetties perched out on wooden stilts over the sea, each with a little red roof at the end. 'It's dead easy,' he said. 'The skipper steers in by them. Never has to use a chart.'

'What are they?' I asked. 'Leading marks?'

'Leading marks?' he said. 'Them's the prison shit-houses!'

In fact, accompanying the Resident Commissioner's secretary aboard to welcome Dick Horton at Tulagi was a gang of 'dark, powerfully built men with hooked noses' who turned out to be convicted murderers. Serving a life sentence in the local jail sometimes entailed porterage duties, and being detailed for launch duty was one of the more popular prison activities.

Suva harbour, where most government officials first arrived, was one of the most impressive sights in the South Pacific. Beyond the red roofs of the warehouses, the jostling stalls of the market, and the weatherboard buildings of the town, the towering coastline of Viti Levu (Great Fiji) encircled the whole bay, as far as the eye could see, in a grape-coloured frieze of peaks and indentations. The poet Rupert Brooke, embarking here in 1913, described them as the most fantastically shaped mountains in the world, reminding him of the coast of hell in Greek mythology.

When Philip Snow first got off the boat in Fiji, the one impression that dominated everything else, in that hot and humid atmosphere, was the smell of copra, the dried flesh of the coconut. It was stacked up in sacks all down the jetty, alongside the ketches and the cutters which had brought them in from the outlying islands. 'I liked it immediately, sweet and cloying and unmistakable.' For most Europeans that smell remained the most evocative single reminder of the islands.

Once on dry land, any white newcomer was immediately the subject of intense interest, as Len Usher discovered when he arrived from New Zealand to take up a teaching post in 1930.

Suva was then not very much more than a village, and there was very little traffic in the streets – an occasional motor car, a few horse-drawn vehicles. I was travelling with another new schoolteacher, a woman, and our ship arrived in the late afternoon. The passenger lists were published in the *Fiji Times* in those days, and by evening everybody in Suva knew who we were.

The High Commission headquarters was in the grounds of Government House in Suva, and newcomers were sometimes invited to spend a few days as a house guest of His Excellency. For Ronald Garvey, it was a stroke of luck that the then Governor had a special predilection for the Oloroso sherry which was a prize product of the Garvey family firm back in England. One way and another, Cadet 26374 was soon sufficiently in favour to be asked to stand in as ADC to His Excellency from time to time.

I was staying in what was a temporary Government House, because the original Government House had recently been burnt down by lightning. Even so, the place was organised on the usual fairly grand scale with lavish dinner parties and all the elegant formalities, the palm trees and the Pacific at our doorstep. There were chauffeurs to run both cars of the private secretaries, there were ADCs, there were masses of servants. After about a week of this sort of thing I came to the conclusion that this quite definitely was the sort of life that I would aim for. Since it seemed a very charming and lovely place, with particularly delightful people, it might not be a bad idea to set my sights on becoming Governor of Fiji. Well, that was 1926. I became Governor of Fiji in 1952 . . .

2
Learning the Ropes

For most new arrivals, their first encounter with local authority – usually the Resident Commissioner, head of government in each island group – could be a daunting experience. In the Gilberts the RC was known to the islanders as the Old Man. His official bungalow was perched on a broad plateau well above sea level on Ocean Island, then the administrative headquarters of the Gilbert and Ellice group. The house could only be approached by climbing up a rough and dusty track for about a mile. It seemed very much longer to Andrew Armstrong, sweltering under the equatorial sun in his obligatory white suit and nervously rehearsing himself for the introduction ahead.

I was received quite formally by the Acting Resident Commissioner and his family, and we had tea. I was rather hoping for something stronger, because I was exhausted by that climb up the hill. Then we went into his study, and he said, 'Now, I want to give you some advice. Firstly, don't believe a word you hear about anybody on this island, particularly about me. Secondly, get everything in writing. Thirdly, never go into the female jail without a witness.'

The exact duties of the probationer cadet were often bewilderingly vague. On Ocean Island, the government office was sited below the Residency and comprised a shabby one-storey edifice propped up on stilts against the hillside. Here the young Armstrong found himself installed the following day.

I hadn't a clue as to what I was supposed to do. I just read files, and I think the first morning a telegram arrived from the High Commission Office in Fiji.

I asked the clerk, a large, beaming islander called Peni, 'What do you do with these telegrams?'

And he said, 'Oh well, you can do what you like with them, sir.'

I thought I could remember what the contents were, so I put it in the rubbish basket. I saw Peni look at me, but I went on reading the files. Then about an hour later I saw him waddle off to the telephone and ring up the wireless station to ask for a repeat of the telegram.

When it arrived I said to him, 'Now what are you going to do with that telegram?'

And he said, 'Well sir, we usually put them on the files.'

That was my first lesson in secretarial duties . . . and in South Sea diplomacy.

Ronald Garvey's first assignment as a servant of Empire was testing in a different way.

Having arrived in the Solomons, I was pitched straight into the Post Office as Protectorate Postmaster. We used to have a mail ship which came up only once every five weeks, delivering something like 200 bags of mail. It stayed in harbour in Tulagi for just twenty-four hours, and in that time, with one native clerk who could just read English, he and I had to sort that mail out into fifty different bags and see that it went off to the outlying islands.

Rather more dramatic was Dick Horton's first official task in the tiny community at Tulagi. He was instructed to destroy the entire money supply of the Solomons Protectorate. The local notes were about to be exchanged for Australian currency, so the complete existing stock, stacked in bundles in the Treasury strong-room, had to be taken out and burned in a large bonfire on the wharf, while the local spectators rubbed their eyes in disbelief.

In the Gilbert and Ellice Islands, Eric Bevington discovered that there were many ways of proving one's worth as an emissary of the Crown.

There was a native feast I had to attend the first night. Paddy MacDonald, who was the Secretary to Government, was the guest of honour. Right in front of us was a huge bonito fish with great eyes staring up at the kerosene lamp hanging overhead. Then the headman ceremoniously stuck his finger in under the bonito's eye (and his fingernail incidentally revealed that he'd had a hard working day), picked the eye out, and gave it to Paddy MacDonald to swallow. Poor old Paddy – his stomach heaved, but he managed to keep it down. To me that was the epitome of duty.

After a couple of weeks spent 'learning the ropes', as it was always termed, in the Resident Commissioner's Office, Horton was sent to take over the government station on the island of Ysabel. The island contained nothing more than a mission station, a few plantations, the usual prison, police barracks and store, and a population of 4000, but its pride and joy was the government office. The island had been without its District Officer since he had gone on leave, so the office was in a state of disuse.

It was a beautiful thatched building on a little promontory, where it got the occasional cool breeze. Inside there was a tremendous iron safe, and law books and files all over the place. The cockroaches had got at the books and there were cobwebs all over the desk. The corporal in charge of the police came up to report that all was well. Then he saluted with a tremendous stamp, just like a guardsman, at which point the safe gracefully collapsed on the floor with a most terrific bang, the rafters came down, the dust came down – everything came down. There we were, in the middle of a district office which had disappeared. Marvellous beginning! White ants had eaten everything in all directions for a whole six months.

David Trench's first task was to be a mining warden.

I knew absolutely nothing about gold-mining. But I was given a certain Corporal Taloi, two or three policemen and a big bag of shillings, and told to go off up to Gold Ridge. There were a lot of Australians around who were supposed to be prospecting, but in fact they were mining. My job was to camp somewhere up there, and stop the depradations of these miners. I remember Major Sanders, who was the Secretary to Government of the time, saying to me, 'You bloody well do whatever Corporal Taloi tells you,' which was very wise of him. And so Taloi and I built ourselves a camp at about 2000 or 3000 feet, and then chased around amongst the hills, trying to catch those gold diggers at it – which of course was quite hopeless. But I learned a lot from Corporal Taloi about living rough in the Solomons.

The art of surviving in bush conditions was one of the first lessons to be learned by new arrivals, as Nick Waddell discovered right at the start.

You took along such gear as you had in a couple of four-gallon petrol cans. You cut the petrol can in half, put a change of clothes inside, and then put the two halves together. You'd take a little tinned food, and maybe biscuits, which are a great standby for hard rations. But you lived fairly well off the land. You also took some money from the government to pay for porters. If you were doing a longer haul, they would expect to be paid something like a shilling a day. But it was all pretty basic.

Waddell also benefited from Major Sanders' stern approach.

Sanders was renowned for testing out his cadets. For my first job he said he wanted me to survey a possible route across to the opposite coast, to Sinarango, where, only a few years before I got there, the people had slaughtered the District Officer and his new cadet. This was my first bush trek and I had with me two corporals, about five or six police, and a few carriers. It was up and down all the way, 3000 feet up and 2000 feet down, then 3000 feet up again. I was crying with agony some of the time.

The first night I was so fast asleep I didn't hear the fracas going on. It transpired that a rather keen missionary had been praying at the bedside of a village chap who had severe malaria. The man obviously couldn't stand the praying any more, so he let loose with an arrow and shot this poor missionary in the backside. I had to enquire into it but there was really little I could say except: 'Bad luck – don't pray so hard next time.' Then on we went.

There were no roads in the Solomons, of course. You went by paths, up slippery, muddy cross-routes, over fallen trees and tangles of vine and bush. Sometimes there was no path even. The chaps had to hack their way through, with no footholds at all. I suppose it was an epic journey but I didn't care for it. At the end of it all, when I got back, I was reprimanded by Sanders for being slow.

For most new arrivals, domestic life was considerably more mundane. Housing itself was often a disappointment, described architecturally as Early Antipodean. In Suva it consisted of dozens of identical-looking, box-like bungalows dotted about a suburban hinterland known in New Zealand parlance as the Domain.

In fact there was a subtle differentiation in style, according to one's official status. Lowly new administrative officers would be allocated the smallest model, known as the Grade Four, which bordered the roadside. Like many other wives, Jane Roth, settling down in Fiji with her husband in the late 1930s, found living conditions something of a let-down.

> When you got senior you got a better house, but they were all really just timber-framed affairs with tongue-and-groove boarding on the outside, and corrugated iron roofs, and nothing more, not even a proper verandah. When it really rained, which was often, you couldn't hear yourself speak. In the 'summer' months, from November to April, they were very very hot, and then when the temperature went down to sixty it was quite chilly.

On the other hand, if, like Nigel Pusinelli, you were posted to the sandy atolls of the Gilberts, the mod cons might be restricted but you had the delightful compensation of a house in the genuine South Sea tradition.

> It had a framework made of pandanus poles, with a thatched roof, and the walls were woven out of the midrib of the coconut leaf. The only thing imported was the concrete floor. The walls only came up waist-high, and above that one just had blinds as shutters. There was a partition in the middle to make two bedrooms, and the living-room and kitchen on one end, and a bathroom off the other end. It was a very pleasant way of life, right on the edge of the sea with the beach below us. We employed one of the local fishermen, who'd go out to do his fishing at night. So you'd go into the kitchen in the early morning and find a whole great flapping fish, still alive, waiting for you. He'd come in before dawn and just popped the prize of the catch in a bucket of water for us.

If you were unmarried and starting out on your career in a remote part of the islands, you would probably be accommodated in something known as the Batch, the local term for the bachelors' quarters, where half a dozen young men would share what often looked like nothing more than an extended cricket pavilion, with a verandah running along the front and partitioned rooms behind. Dick Horton remembers his particular Batch as 'a barrack-like bungalow, horribly hot and airless'. Equipment in those pre-war years was basic, and even an ice-box was an unheard-of luxury.

> I never saw ice in my drinks for years. But we did have a contraption which kept food fresh for a short time at least. It was a magnificent thing called an Icy-Ball. It consisted of two balls, about the size of footballs, connected by an arched tube

on top. I don't know the mechanics of it, but it took all the heat out of a special insulated cabinet and left it really cold – for a short time at least.

But they were temperamental things. A friend of mine down the corridor had a brand-new Icy-Ball, and one morning there was a most almighty report. The thing had completely blown up. There were bits in the ceilings, bits on the floor, bits of it everywhere. My friend said to me, in a classic phrase, 'Afraid I ballsed it up, didn't I?'

According to the popular idea of South Sea life, any unattached young white man would immediately find himself an object of amorous pursuit by swarms of nubile Polynesian maidens in Dorothy Lamour sarongs and garlands of hibiscus, while guitars strummed softly under the palm trees. Once again, real life was rather different. Ronald Garvey at twenty-four may have exchanged 'a few coy glances' with the chief's eighteen-year-old daughter Tanualoa on a visit to the beautiful island of Utupua, but he was under no illusions about the effects that any affair with a local girl would have had on his career prospects.

From a British point of view, there was a distinctly puritanical attitude towards that sort of thing. In my young days in Fiji, it was called 'mat fever'. Mat fever was going to bed on a Fiji mat with a Fiji girl. It was certainly not regarded as the thing to do if you wanted to get on in the service.

This attitude dated back to earlier days, as Philip Snow discovered while working as private secretary to the Governor of Fiji in 1939. 'To my great delight, early on in my days in Fiji, I found a long-buried circular from the Colonial Office. It was marked "Confidential", dated 1909, and was from the Marquess of Crewe, Secretary of State for the Colonies, Downing Street.'

It has been brought to my notice that officers in the service of some of the Crown Colonies and Protectorates have in some instances entered into arrangements of concubinage with girls and women belonging to the native population of the territories in which they were performing their duties. These illicit connections have at times been a cause of trouble with native populations. Another objection, equally serious from the standpoint of government, lies in the fact that it is not possible for any member of the administration to countenance such practices without lowering himself in the eyes of the natives, and diminishing his authority over them.

Decades later, there was the story of a certain District Commissioner who recommended that every new officer should be provided with a refrigerator and a native woman.

'A native woman?' queried his startled subordinate.

'To look after the fridge, of course!' the DC shouted back.

Robert Lever, who went out to the Solomons as a government entomologist in the 1930s, noticed a tradition of practical assistance in other matters, too.

It was customary to think that members of the administration learnt their languages from native women. So far as I'm concerned this didn't happen. But in other parts the slang for a young lady who aided in that way was a 'brown-backed dictionary'. Whether such a form of reference could be relied upon for grammar or syntax, I would not like to say.

From the islanders' point of view, there was a complex code of custom to be observed. Marriages were arranged by parents, and the virgin daughters of land-owning families were a valuable commodity. In the Micronesian society of the Gilberts, though, Eric Bevington noticed convenient loopholes in the system on both sides.

You were only bound by native custom. If you transgressed native custom and got into trouble, then headquarters would get very angry with you. But there were District Officers who availed themselves of the local ladies' comforts. As it happens, I was engaged to be married to a young woman in England, with whom I was deeply in love. But I did hear natives say on many occasions what peculiar people we British were. Here were these beautiful girls, unmarried girls who were available. It had nothing to do with prostitution. The Gilbertese word for them means 'the leftovers'. They were usually slightly past marriageable age, which was the early twenties. They probably had no land to put into the marriage, and land was absolutely vital, so they had become the leftovers. The Gilbertese thought we must be a bit odd if we didn't take them on. One of my colleagues did. He's no longer alive, but it was nothing against him at all. I think he was twelve years alone in one group of islands. Well, I mean, he'd have been a nutcase if he hadn't taken unto him a local woman.

The pressures of loneliness were made even greater by the strict Colonial Office ruling that no administrative officer could marry during his first spell of duty, which might last for between three and six years. Above all, it was essential to be confirmed in one's post before such a privilege might be granted. Confirmation in its turn depended on passing a variety of stiff examinations, including local language and custom, as well as something called General and Financial Orders and Colonial Regulations. But, as Eric Bevington relates, when extenuating circumstances were held to apply, government sometimes showed mercy.

I got some sort of phosphate poisoning, because I was in a low state, and all my skin started peeling off. They found the cure to that, but it meant an unpleasant five weeks on my back. Then my superiors – God bless them – formed the opinion that it was all due to malnutrition, and I didn't look after myself. The Secretary to Government had been to my house and said I didn't have proper meals and that sort of thing. I had made tentative enquiries to ask if I couldn't possibly get married within the six years, and they decided that I should and could. In fact, many years later in Fiji, in the High Commission Office, I saw the official minute in which it said that this young man is quite promising, but doesn't feed himself properly, and to have a wife to feed him and look after him would probably be a good investment. So I got permission to marry. I was very, very lucky. By and large, you were simply not allowed to marry on your first tour.

Philip Snow was also lucky enough to be made an exception to the rule. It was at the time of the outbreak of the Second World War; all leave had been cancelled and he was particularly anxious for his fiancée in England to be allowed to join him in Fiji. A kindly Governor, Sir Harry Luke, although himself a bachelor, gave his blessing to the proposal, and in April 1940 Miss Anne Harris undertook the long and perilous sea journey out to become Mrs Snow.

I certainly didn't take out a white wedding dress with me. Our idea was that we should be married very quietly in a register office and have a few friends to a drink afterwards at the hotel. None of it in fact turned out like that. I arrived in Suva at half past seven in the morning and I was taken by Philip more or less immediately to meet Sir Harry Luke. I well remember that first breakfast at Government House on the balcony overlooking

Suva harbour with the lawns and tropical gardens below. It was absolutely marvellous.

Sir Harry Luke completely took over and said, 'Nonsense, you must be married in the cathedral.' The gardener at Government House made up a bouquet of white frangipani for me. I was married in just a plain summer suit, and Philip was in a lounge suit. The only person in anything different was the Chief Justice, who turned up in a morning suit, and everyone thought he was the bridegroom. I was given away by a complete stranger, another government official. The ceremony was at five o'clock in Suva Pro-cathedral, and the reception was immediately afterwards – very grand, at Government House. I didn't know a soul there, except for my husband. I remember Sir Harry Luke made a joke about my being the only person to stay at GH who had occupied a single room and a double room in the same day. He invited us to stay on for our honeymoon, and we spent the next three days there as his guests. Then it was time to set sail for our first home at Lomaloma in the Lau Islands.

The war in Europe was a very long way away. The Japanese invasion of the Pacific was yet to come. For that brief moment, the islands were still peacefully cocooned in the calm of another era. It was a world without tourism, without politics, without real poverty. In a setting of such immense natural beauty, inhabited by a people who seemed to have a gift for happiness, it must have appeared a gilded view indeed from the verandahs of Government House.

3
The Customs of the Chiefs

For the British, the sheer geographical scale of the Pacific Empire was a bewildering experience. So was the contrast in race and custom from group to group. A million square miles of ocean encompassed the Gilberts alone, while Fiji, the administrative hub of the whole network of British dependencies, included 300 islands of every shape and size. Lomaloma, destination of Philip and Anne Snow after their Suva wedding, was a truly Polynesian outpost, on the easternmost fringe of the Fiji group. For centuries it had been dominated by the neighbouring Tongans, and in the 1860s and 1870s it was the power base of the wily Tongan prince Ma'afu. At that time it was also an important trading station and port of entry. Ma'afu's government was modelled on European lines, right down to his police force with their red, white and blue uniforms and peaked caps bearing the word 'ovisa' (officer), while he himself presided over his General Assembly in white ducks and black morning coat. But fifty years later, Lomaloma was a quiet backwater again, and for Anne Snow it was a life of almost complete isolation from European society.

> There were only three other Europeans, a copra planter and his wife, and the owner of the local store who had the odd name of Umphrey – Thomas Oswald Umphrey Stockwell. We became great friends with Mr Stockwell, who had been around the islands all his life. We used to go down there to drink his home brew every evening and listen to the news, because we didn't have a wireless set and he did, of a sort. The brew was beer, pretty strong I think, and it wasn't very long before Philip had stones put along the beach from the bottom of the path up to our house to Thomas Oswald Umphrey Stockwell's house. He had the stones painted white, and of course the Fijians teased us and said they knew the real reason why this was done – because it made it so much easier for us to find our way back after drinking the home brew!

At twenty-five, Philip Snow found himself District Commissioner for the whole of the Lau group. Both the Snows became, as they say, Fijianised and Tonganised. They ate the island food, and spoke the local dialect – Anne Snow later became the first European woman to pass the government examination in the Fijian which she had learned in Lomaloma. She was only twenty on her arrival there, and her twenty-first birthday was celebrated in Polynesian style when the Snows held open house for almost the whole of the local population, with the traditional songs and dances and a feast to follow.

Economically it was a slump period for the islands and copra, the principal crop, had fallen to a mere £1 a ton, too low in value to be anything but barter for stores. But hard times rarely affected the famous Fijian *joie de vivre*. On a more sedate level, the social event that lay at the heart of all village life was the nightly *yanggona* circle at the chief's house. The government officer was always welcome in the circle, and for John Goepel these lamplit gatherings touched a special chord in the imagination.

> I found that living in the Fijian villages was exactly like Homer. In the evening they all gathered in the big house and we'd have the *yanggona* – that's the national drink – passed round in coconut cups to each in turn. And if you look in any bit of the *Odyssey* that's exactly what happened: the chief was there and the cup went round and they told stories – tales of the great days and the old heroes of the Golden Age.

As to the virtues of the drink itself, made from the root of a Pacific pepper plant (*Piper methysticum*), opinions varied. Ronald Paine, who arrived in Fiji in 1925 as a government entomologist, pinned it down as 'A mixture of Sanitas and tea. It had an astringent flavour, and it made one want to smoke.' 'Rather like indigestion mixture,' was how Charis Coode found it, touring the islands as the wife of an administrative officer. 'Quite refreshing, though, especially on a hot day if you'd been travelling.'

By custom, *yanggona* is drunk from a coconut shell and must be drained at a gulp. Graham Leggatt, English master at Queen Victoria School – the Eton of Fiji – had no doubt as to the potency of the beverage, after he had been on a tour of the main island with some of his senior Fijian pupils.

> I had never drunk *yanggona* at that stage, but one evening the boys got someone to bring me some and I drank a bit of it. The following day on the bus I was unwise enough to say, 'I don't

know why you make all that fuss about the stuff. It's just like drinking water – has absolutely no effect at all.' So the following night they arranged to get me! The chap who was handing out the *yanggona* had instructions to keep bringing it to me. I found that eventually it had a weird effect on your co-ordination. It leaves your brain absolutely clear. You can think perfectly well. But you have difficulty in speaking or moving. I was trying to dance and my legs weren't functioning properly. So eventually, when it came to me next, I said 'No thanks,' and a great cry went up round the hall: 'He's had enough!' Two of the prefects escorted me back to the house where I was to sleep, and as I stumbled in the darkness I heard this wicked chuckle behind me and a voice saying 'Oh, so it's like water, is it, sir?'

The formal serving of *yanggona* was a very different matter, a complex ritual of welcome and respect, which was also accorded to all European visitors of status. For an outsider, it could be a somewhat intimidating occasion. First there was the intense silence, reminiscent of the sacred invocations of the old days, when a movement across the string of cowrie shells tied to the bowl, a mistake in the order of serving, could mean instant death or a large-scale war. In those days the root was pulped by chewing. The twentieth-century visitor was always relieved to find it ground and ready in the bowl. But every stage was full of solemnity – the two young warriors pouring water from long pipes of bamboo, the low droning chant from the circle of elders. For ten minutes you sat and watched as the master of ceremonies strained and squeezed the mixture through a bunch of hibiscus fibres. Then with a flourish he threw the bundle of fibres over his shoulder. Treading soft as a panther, the cup-bearer, rustling in his kilt of crimson leaves, crouched to receive the first serving, then carried the bowl slowly across to the guest of honour, knees still flexed and muscled arms outstretched. Eyes flickered white in the mask-like faces of the onlookers. Their scrutiny had almost the quality of hypnotism. Only the cry of '*Matha*' (empty), and the hand-claps released the spring of tension as you sent the cup spinning back across the mat in the approved fashion.

District Officer might be a humble title in the hierarchy of the Colonial Office, but to the rural Fijians you were the representative of the Crown itself, as John Goepel discovered.

They would give me all sorts of things because I counted as a great chief. When I arrived in a place, they came along with whale's teeth, which were the traditional tokens of good faith, and twenty-four turtles, say, and three bullocks roasted whole, and twelve pigs, and so on. The chief's herald would approach me, turning his face away and squatting down on his hunkers. Then, giving the three claps that were the sign of respect, he would say in Fijian, 'We have a small offering.'

And all the people on my side would say, '*Levu, levu!*' (A very big one, very big one!). It was the polite thing for a gift to be made little of by the donor and made much of by the recipient. Then I would say, 'Accept it,' and my own herald would go up and call out in a sort of sing-song voice, 'I accept this offering from the people of Namosi (or wherever it was). Long live the Government, long live the King and people of Namosi!' After that I would say, 'Let it be divided among those present.'

A huge sigh of relief would go up. They'd put it all out in baskets and spread it on the village green for every tribe to come and collect, and everyone would go home happy. That was the Fijian way.

Business had a way of merging into pleasure before you knew it, especially when the women took charge. John Goepel recalls presiding over the democratically elected provincial council in the usual thatched meeting house at the centre of the village.

Suddenly there was a shout from outside and fifty women came in in a procession. I remember each one was wearing a brilliant, electric-blue dress made from some kind of trade-store calico. This reached to the ground and over it came a wrapper of *tapa* – that's native barkcloth – highly ornamented. They had feathers and flowers in their hair, and each one was carrying a basket of fruit, and we said, 'No, no! Not now! We're in the middle of a council meeting. This is the House of Parliament sitting.' They took not the slightest notice. They walked in, they sat down in rows and they performed those lovely Fijian hand-dances for an hour, and we just had to accept it. I mean you can't spoil a women's party for a little thing like a parliamentary session.

John Goepel, who was an accomplished pianist, got to know the island songs and found the Fijian repertoire remarkably varied.

There were three kinds of song, really. There were the old Fijian compositions which went with their dances – long chants with a drop of the voice at the end, and I couldn't get that down in any kind of notation that I knew, however hard I tried. Then there were the imported American songs. One favourite we all used to sing was, 'Show Me the Way to Go Home', in English,

Fijian and Hindustani. Then there were sentimental Fijian songs with really beautiful words that could have been written in late Victorian times.

The young entomologist, Ronald Paine, was another connoisseur of Fijian music. Although his professional brief was the liquidation of the Levuana Leaf Moth, the Coconut Spike Moth and other enemies of the copra plantations, he still had time to compile several notebooks of words and music on his travels. He too would bring out his ukelele wherever he went, often with a couple of his contemporaries to complete the act.

During the two years after I arrived in Fiji, first Harley Nott came out, and then a year later Ronald Garvey. We were all Cambridge men and the three of us styled ourselves The Cantab Trio. We used to go round singing ribald songs, accompanied by two of us on ukeleles and Ronald Garvey with his guitar. Our technique was not very good – busking, you'd call it now – but we had great fun. We used to get Fijians, who were very competent with guitars, to come and sing with us. They are natural musicians and they have a wonderful sense of harmony. So we learned all their songs and they learned ours.

Most of the English found that the pattern of life in the Fijian countryside had a charm all its own. Work in the food plots or plantations was allotted daily by the village headman. Sunset and the sound of the *lali* drum brought everyone home together, the men with bunches of yams and bananas slung on yokes across their shoulders, the girls with their firewood strapped to their backs or laden with nets and baskets of fish, a hump-backed procession against the flaring sky. Woodsmoke mingled with the brief violet-coloured dusk, and oil lamps glimmered in open doorways. There was the smell of coconut oil and sandalwood, rubbed on after the evening bathe, and ahead stretched the long, gregarious Fijian evening.

Apart from the traditional dances, a great favourite in all the villages was an importation called the *taralala*. It was a kind of Polynesian palais glide, sedately performed by couples linked side by side, with an arm around each other's waist, who circled the wooden floor like the spokes of a wheel, with a hurricane lamp at the centre. Accompaniment was a sing-song of some kind, with the ubiquitous guitar or ukelele, but there was a special ritual about the way partners were selected. Any young District Officer who felt his foot tapped gently by a shadowy figure on her knees before him had no recourse but to jump up and join the dance. The *taralala* had the usual Fijian quality of being infinitely prolonged. So had another village pastime, at which John Goepel became something of an expert.

In my early days before I had any authority, it was all much more fun. They taught me to play what they call *lafo*, which is a kind of giant shove ha'penny. You played it on a mat about fifteen foot long, and you folded the sides underneath. It was a rush mat, stiffish, so that you made a kind of valley all the way up. Then you folded the end underneath too. For counters, we used *ivi* nuts – they're about two inches across, like horse chestnuts but flat, just half an inch thick. The game is to get your counter as near as possible to the end, without going over the edge. You're allowed to knock the other man's off, just like shove ha'penny, or put stoppers down in front of yours, like in bowls. And you'd throw your *lafo* up and try and get as near to the edge as possible. Apparently, when coinage was first introduced into Fiji, they thought, 'Oh, the ideal thing for playing *lafo* with!' So coins were called *lafo* – the word for money is the same as for shove ha'penny counters. It says quite a lot about the Fijians.

These were the District Officer's times of relaxation. But while on duty he had his official dignity to uphold, something which applied even to the arrival of the morning mail.

In my district in Bua, I was sitting in my office the first day and I heard the *tama*. That's a kind of roar the people make to salute a chief. The next minute the postman came in – on all fours of course, with his face nicely averted from the radiance of my countenance. Still keeping his face away, he handed me a letter, sat down on his haunches and clapped three times as the final sign of respect, and disappeared backwards.

While they were living and travelling in the rough conditions of the interior, though, there were bound to be certain moments when loss of face was unavoidable.

I was getting to a village and the approach was over a very deep, muddy creek, crossed by a single coconut log. I started walking across this in my shoes, because in Fijian eyes Europeans are traditionally the 'Boot-Wearers'. Now, a Fijian walks across a coconut log, walks up a coconut tree, with his bare feet and his toes clinging on. But I wasn't so good at that, so I kept my shoes on, and halfway across this muddy swaying log I was in danger of falling off. There was only one thing to do. I dropped on my hands and knees, and finished the journey into the village that way, while the schoolchildren were lined up in two rows, boys on one side, girls on the other, singing 'God Save the King'.

Most of the time the administrative officer was performing a balancing act of another kind, walking a tightrope between familiarity and isolation, as far as his relations with the local people were concerned. It was a compromise that some found far from easy to strike. But John Goepel discovered that the Fijians' own distinction between chiefs and commoners sometimes helped to simplify matters.

Some situations could be very embarrassing because you were the headmaster the whole time, talking to the class. The headmaster can't get too friendly with his pupils, and they don't want to get too friendly with him. With the chief, it was different. You behaved as one in authority to another, and some of the chiefs were of an extremely high standard. A great friend of mine was Ratu Veli, a very nice person. His grandfather was one of the chiefs who'd signed the Deed of Cession, and when I was staying with him once he said, 'I'd like you to have this wooden headrest that belonged to my grandfather.'

I said, 'Veli, I can't take that. It's a family heirloom, it's much too valuable. It's historic.'

He said, 'Well, if I don't give it to you, I shall only give it to someone who doesn't appreciate it.'

Ratu Veli was as ingenious as he was generous. He got a message once that the government auditor was arriving the next day to inspect the accounts. I saw him turn a faint green underneath his brown. But he soon recovered himself and sent down to a Chinese store a message to let him have £70 or whatever it was. The Chinaman sent it up, the auditor came the next day, counted the cash, and said, 'Ratu Veli, the money is quite right but you've got rather a lot of silver. You ought to get rid of some of it.'

So Veli said, 'Certainly I will.' And he sent it all back to the Chinaman next day.

The British found qualities in the Fijian character that irritated – unreliability and lack of drive were favourite charges. But as far as Eric Bevington was concerned, there was little doubt as to the outcome of any comparison between the two races: 'South Sea islanders are nature's gentlemen. They have a code of conduct and ethics that in many ways is far superior to our own, and we call ourselves civilised.'

Even apart from these echoes of eighteenth-century enthusiasm for the Noble Savage, there did seem to exist a special kind of relationship between the British and the Fijians. It struck Philip Snow right from the start: 'I always felt that there was a natural rapport between Fijian character and British character. Their sense of humour is so similar to ours, and I think we appreciate the same sort of values – good manners, a calm temperament, combined with an extrovert conviviality.' As a result, many close and enduring friendships were formed between those who were able to meet on an equal footing, in particular the chiefs and the administrators.

In the 1920s and 1930s, the outstanding chief was Ratu Sir Lala Sukuna, named from the English word 'schooner', who had a gift for such friendships. His personal kindness to Len Usher was responsible for the young man's decision to settle in Fiji for good.

Ratu Sukuna was without doubt the foremost Fijian chief of his generation, an extraordinary man. He was the first Fijian to go overseas to school. He was the first Oxford student from Fiji and the first Oxford graduate. Then, when war broke out in 1914, he found that his colour was against him and he was not acceptable to the British army. So he crossed the Channel and joined the French Foreign Legion. He won the Médaille Militaire, which is the French equivalent of the Victoria Cross. He then came back to Fiji and, working his way up the administrative ladder, occupied practically all the high offices open to a civil servant. His great gift was that he was a man of two worlds, who was able to interpret the Fijian people to Europeans and Indians, and to interpret them in turn to the Fijians.

For some reason he took me under his wing when I first met him in 1932. He said to me, 'You spend some time with me, and I will show you Fiji.' From then on, I used to spend all my holidays with him, and when he came to Suva to live, I formed the habit of seeing him every lunchtime, and spending every Sunday afternoon with him.

Then I said to him one day that I was thinking of getting married. The next day he came along and told me, 'I was talking to Maria' – that was his wife – 'about your wedding last night. I think we'll have about fifty guests, maybe a few more. We're going to look after this wedding.' My wedding invitations went out: 'Ratu Sukuna and Andi Maria request the pleasure of the company of . . .' and so on.

Then later, when I told him that my wife was going to have a baby, he said, 'Right-o, I claim the privilege of a Fijian chief, and I will name the child. He or she is to have my name, Lala. And it doesn't matter if it's a boy or a girl – Lala will suit both.' And so my eldest daughter bears the name of the great Sukuna.

For Philip Snow, whose daughter also had a Fijian name bestowed on her by Ratu Sukuna, it was especially disturbing to discover the existence of racial barriers, not only in the sugar towns where the Australian refining company was dominant, but on the main cricket field of the capital.

When I first went there in 1938, I was totally surprised to see that Europeans and part-Europeans were playing on one part of Albert Park, which is a large and splendid ground, and on the other part there would be Fijians and Indians. I couldn't see the logic or the reason for this differentiation at all. I was made secretary of the Suva Cricket Club almost as soon as I got out there, and from this position I was able to enlist the support of some of the more liberal-minded Europeans. They agreed that it was high time that all the races should be amalgamated in one competition, and this was done. I was unpopular with a few Europeans after this for quite a while – to my surprise. But I never regretted it, and we were able to form the national team which was to tour the world with such success.

The whole structure and ethos of *Kirikiti* fascinated the Fijians. Exuberant eleven-a-side dances commemorated peak moments in the inter-tribal matches. Rival teams were distinguished by their fantastic haircuts, and in the early 1900s, government officers such as St Johnston were recording waves of cricket madness that had to be checked by law. Outlying villages would keep up a match of forty or fifty a side for weeks on end. In his book *Cricket in the Fiji Islands*, Philip Snow records the typical reaction of a Fijian batsman on being bowled or caught out, his undisguised misery, 'walking with trailing bat and feet back to the pavilion'. There were also other national characteristics of play.

They wouldn't mind bowling, although it didn't seem quite as dignified a process as batting. They liked batting very much. But fielding they thought was very definitely the job of commoners. So when it came to the turn of the Fijian side to have to field, the chiefs would make themselves absent and leave all the hard work to the commoners. They're of course very strong people, and they hit the ball as hard as they possibly can when they're batting and they bowl as fast as they possibly can when they're bowling, and they think there's something wrong with your arm if you're a slow bowler. But their natural exuberance and zest made their game not just stylish, but spectacular.

4
Signing the Book

Although each island group had its Resident Commissioner and its Residency, Government House in Fiji was the peak of protocol, the social mecca for every young administrator from the outposts. Government House itself was an elegant phoenix that arose from the ashes of a 1920s lightning strike. Its sweeping drives and white colonnades, copied from Government House, Ceylon, were for the British a cherished token of the Raj-style glories of Empire, rarely experienced in the Pacific.

After the mandatory signing of the visitors' book, the invitation to dinner would arrive, involving black tie, butterfly collar and bum-freezer – the tropical white jacket cut just below the waist. A silk cummerbund, another import from India, completed the ensemble. By tradition, every colonial territory had its official colour – green for Nigeria, red for Sierra Leone, gold for the Gold Coast. It was something of a disappointment to young cadets to find that Fiji had been designated plain black cummerbunds. Only a Governor or an official of rank had the sartorial confidence to appear, as happened occasionally, in a barkcloth cummerbund emblazoned with Polynesian patterns of cream and brown.

To Philip Snow it seemed that the only outlet left for the expression of personality was the tie. His choice for an official ball, a multi-coloured striped bow-tie, was the insignia of a well-known Cambridge drinking club. The Governor's gaze was stony, and next day Snow was left in little doubt as to His Excellency's opinion of his choice. 'Never wear that thing again! Utterly flamboyant!'

Sir Harry Luke, the Excellency in question, was ironically enough one of Fiji's most flamboyant Governors. He was also a famous host, and dinner at Government House was sufficiently glorious to wipe out any personal blot on one's copybook – banks of purple Fijian orchids glowing in the lamplight down the long table, a turbaned bearer behind each chair. In those days Indians were chosen as servants in preference to Fijians, who were regarded as too exuberant for the discipline required. Otherwise Fijian culture was evident everywhere, a practice begun in the 1870s by Sir Arthur Gordon, who went so far as to appear barefoot on official occasions, despite resulting ulcers, and insisted that his retinue did likewise. Fifty years later, dinner was announced by the sound of the same *lali* drum, and the walls bristled with an awesome array of pineapple clubs, whale's teeth and polished spears.

There was entertaining night life too in the streets of the capital, at the wharfside bars and *kava* saloons in All Nations Street, and on the hospitable verandahs of a dozen hotels. To Andrew Armstrong, 'It was a metropolis – it was like going to New York. Absolutely astounding after the isolation of the Gilbert and Ellice.'

Sometimes the young visitor might be accorded the honour of being invited to stay at Government House. This meant that visits to the town would have to be curtailed and the house regime respected, as Armstrong recalls.

I was bidden to stay for five days by this rather austere Governor, Sir Murchison Fletcher. He was a very kindly person, but he was very stiff, very brisk, too. There was usually a large party at lunch or dinner and I was very junior. I was always put down the end of the table. His Excellency was always served first and started at once, and he ate at a great rate. By the time the servants got round to me I had a real job to try and keep up. Usually I was only halfway through the course when the plates were removed. All my life I've eaten much too quickly, and I attribute this solely to staying at Government House. I've heard other people say the same thing.

Local delicacies were always featured on the Government House menus. The asparagus-like *nduruka*, dressed in coconut cream, *kokonda* – raw fish marinated in lime juice – fresh mangoes, huge prawns and delicate land crabs were particularly popular. Less so were the *mbalolo*, the sea-worms served like whitebait by some more adventurous Governors' ladies.

Suva was also the headquarters of the Western Pacific High Commission, so there were respects to be paid by visiting young administrators to superior officers, and, most important of all, calling cards must be left at the homes of senior hostesses. There were dinner parties at the Grand Pacific Hotel, of Somerset Maugham fame. With its palm-fringed verandahs and genuine Palm Court orchestra, it was a considerable cut above the other hostelries of the capital, as Len Usher remembers.

If you dined at the Grand Pacific Hotel on a Saturday night, you would certainly be expected to wear a black tie, dinner jacket and so on, however hot it might be. I did think things might be more relaxed at the Metropole, which was one of those old-fashioned weatherboard buildings where things could be fairly rough. The main feature of the hotel was the saloon bar, which was rather like something out of the old Westerns. But I was sitting in the lounge when the proprietor came along and tapped me on the shoulder. 'Six o'clock, old man,' he said. I didn't know what he meant until he indicated my clothing. It was very hot and I was in my shirtsleeves, but once the sun went down this was out of the question. 'Coat and tie, old man,' he said. 'Coat and tie.' Goodness gracious me! In the Metropole now, I don't think anybody has ever seen a tie!

In the 1920s, though, even daytime wear had its formalities.

I wore white duck trousers, white shirt and jacket. If it was very hot I would perhaps discard the jacket. But shorts for men were certainly not the thing. You wore formal starched clothing, and although it was cheap to have made – a full suit was less than £4 – laundry cost at least fifteen shillings or a pound a month, and of course in that climate you produced quite a lot of laundry. Fijians wore the *sulu* much more frequently then. It was a wrap-around skirt, just a piece of patterned cloth which they wound round themselves and then tucked the ends in at the waist, or sometimes it could be a tailored affair fastened by buckles and buttons – very smart, too.

Much as Europeans might envy the practical coolness of this garment, to an expatriate the *sulu* was only permissible as night attire. Indeed, it was the mark of the seasoned South Sea resident to sip your final whisky with your wrap of flowered calico tucked round your waist as you stretched out on your verandah with friends.

On the whole, though, it was important that standards should not be seen to slip. Ronald Garvey, marooned in an outpost of the Solomons, took good care to have his hair cut by the only 'barber' available, an Australian lumberjack. The result was a shaven head in the best convict tradition. Unfortunately an official visit to Suva was looming, and in order to redress the balance the desperate Garvey grew a beard. By Suva standards this was even worse, and friends who met him off the boat were appalled at the sight of him.

People from the office who were waiting for me took one look at me and said, 'Good God, Ronald – you know you've got to meet the High Commissioner at ten o'clock! You can't go and see him in that!'

I said, 'Really? Well, what had I better do?'

They said, 'Shave it off, for goodness sake. Shave it off at once. I mean, you don't get asked to meet the High Commissioner very often. Better make as good an impression as you can.'

So then and there, back in the cabin, I pulled out a blunt razor, and I can even now feel the grim horror of tearing off a beard which was quite well-rooted by then, so that I could arrive before my High Commissioner, Sir Murchison Fletcher, clean-shaven, and with some propect of a career before me.

Once outside the formal atmosphere of the capital, the assortment of titles bestowed even on an unconfirmed cadet had a distinctly Gilbert and Sullivan flavour – District Officer, District Commissioner, Magistrate, Superintendent of Gaols, Officer-in-charge of Police, Receiver of Wrecks and more, depending on the size of the local establishment. An administrative officer was also the Sub-Accountant, according to Philip Snow 'a not very edifying title' for what involved a great deal of work as the District Treasurer, who was responsible for the collecting of taxes and revenue, as well as payments for leases, usually by Indians to their Fijian landlords. As an administrative officer you might also be appointed Deputy Sheriff, a title that went well with the usual tin-roof office and the lounging figures on the weatherboard verandahs of the dusty main street.

As regards the everyday round of work, most would agreed with Philip Snow that two things had to be remembered.

First, to be always accessible. Office hours were flexible, but we lived on the government station so that anyone could come to the house, front or back door, whenever they chose, at all hours – as they frequently did. Second, to tour the district – being seen was as important as to see. There was no real substitute for that personal contact and knowledge.

Physically covering your district could present problems, especially if you were posted around the hill country of Vanua Levu, Fiji's second largest island, as John Goepel was.

In my first district, I had two horses. I kept one horse on the station and the other fifteen miles north. Then sometimes I had to go along the south coast where there were three ranges of hills that went up to about 1000 feet. The first time I tried it with a horse, the horse stumbled and threw me. I cracked my hip on a boulder and nearly crippled myself, so I never took the horse there again. I used to prefer to walk the thirty miles.

Sea travel could sometimes seem almost as risky. Getting around the district usually meant hopping aboard whatever craft was available, sometimes a natty government vessel with brass gleaming and official flags flying, but more often a banana boat bulging with islanders and their belongings, including a few friendly pigs and goats, or one of the local copra schooners, well known for their cockroaches and their 'roll' in bad weather. Picturesque crews, and skippers straight out of Conrad, could prove alarmingly casual about the technicalities of steering a course through waters that were still only sketchily charted. Every coast was threaded with hidden reefs. For District Commissioner Quentin Weston a visit to Rotuma, the northernmost outpost of the Fiji group, was an adventurous interlude in his ordinary round of duties. But the return journey of some 500 miles, via the Yasawa Islands, was rather more adventurous than he had bargained for.

It wasn't exactly a good beginning. We embarked on the return journey with all ten crew down with flu, including the captain and the cook. It was very stormy, but I thought all would be well because we had a very reliable Fijian skipper called Vuki in charge. But because it was in what we call foreign waters, Rotuma being outside Fiji itself, you have to have someone in charge with a foreign master's ticket. So we had taken on board a man called Captain Anderson, who was a very heavy drinker. He insisted upon a certain course which Vuki said was not correct, shaking his head to himself in that Fijian way. But Vuki was under his control.

A few days later we were getting close to the Yasawas and most of the crew were still sick. Thinking that I ought to play my part, I went up to take the wheel in the early hours of the morning. I was keen on sailing, but I had never taken the wheel of a boat like that before – a big heavy thing with terrific sails. After I'd done a reasonable stint some not too sick member of the crew took over, and then at one o'clock in the morning we went aground on the reef. The weather was even rougher now, and we certainly got a battering. The boat filled up with water. As luck would have it we were just opposite the tiny little island of Viwa, which was suffering from a long drought, and had very little water. With the dawn all these people from Viwa came to rescue us in their canoes, and they were very pleased to see our enormous cargo of oranges, which were floating around in the water. After they'd picked us up these people from Viwa spent hours fishing them all out in nets. They made a very good substitute for water.

From December to March was the hurricane season. John Goepel never forgot the experience of his first hurricane.

There was a big mango tree in front of us. The rain was coming absolutely horizontally and so thick you couldn't see anything beyond. A minute later we looked up again and the tree wasn't there. It had just gone. Then the rain stopped and I went out and had a look round the house. It all looked pretty shaky but still in one piece. Then to my dismay it started blowing again, but from the opposite direction. This was what a hurricane did, once its centre had passed. But I didn't know that. It was not till next day that it all died down. The river rose down in the town and came up about five feet inside the local store. The worst thing was it washed all the labels off the tins, so after that they were selling 'tins unspecified' at threepence each. I bought a whole lot, and I remember opening goodness knows how many tins of jam when I was looking for a tin of bully beef, and all the while I was starving!

Crops and villages in the rural areas were sometimes damaged on a disastrous scale, but the effects of even a moderate hurricane could be seen in the capital, where Jane Roth lived. 'The strangest thing is that all the leaves are stripped off the trees, so that having battened yourself down with luxuriant tropical gardens outside, when the hurricane's over and you go out it looks like England in midwinter.'

Irma Forbes, wife of the Resident Magistrate, was living in Suva in a typical wooden house raised a couple of feet above the ground. During a hurricane, this provided shelter for some strangely assorted refugees.

The first thing I saw was the cat collecting her kittens and putting them under the house. She wouldn't come inside. Then round the other side we noticed a huge flock of mynah birds and they all came in under the house too, which they didn't normally do. Then we ourselves battened down and the storm raged. In the middle of a hurricane everything goes absolutely dead silent. We ventured on to the verandah, looking out and wondering whether the tree next door was going to come down on our neighbour's house, when we saw one solitary mynah bird come out. He looked up, realised the hurricane was coming from the other direction, and shot back underneath. So we dashed back inside and sat it out, too!

Far less devastating was the occasional small earthquake or series of earth tremors. Like many newcomers Graham Leggatt, then teaching at Suva Grammar School, had never associated Fiji with earthquakes, which made his particular experience all the more alarming.

The boys were still on holiday but I was upstairs in the school hostel which was a concrete building. There was a tremendous bang. I realised that the ceiling was moving, the whole building was shaking and the windows were rattling like mad. I had a little drinks cabinet with cocktail glasses on top of it, and I could see them hopping across and smashing on the floor, and I was mentally ticking off each ten and sixpence – idiotic really, but in a situation like that you don't know what to do. Eventually I ran, and by the time I got outside the quake had stopped.

Everything seemed very still, except you could hear the palm leaves rattling overhead. We were right beside the sea and next to us was the Suva Bowling Green, a very elite institution in those days. We were all standing there rather stunned, and one of the school servants, an Indian, walked across the bowling green to take a look out to sea. Whereupon some old duffer came out and shouted to him, 'Get off the bowling green! Get off the bowling green immediately!' I always remember that – it was so absurd.

But before we could react, someone yelled out, 'Run for your lives, it's a tidal wave!' We could see this huge wave coming in, not once but several times. Apparently the water came up to ten feet inside the school, and of course it absolutely submerged the bowling green. The Fijians had the right idea. They just waited for the wave to recede and then rushed across scooping up armfuls of fish that were lying stranded all over the green. A terrific haul they got. That was something that would never have occurred to a European.

A few hundred yards further along the front were the gardens of Government House. Patricia Garvey, wife of the then Governor, Sir Ronald Garvey, was born in Fiji and well used to the violence of the island weather. But even for her, that particular tidal wave was a vivid episode, starting with the quake itself.

I was shopping and I felt it as I was getting out of the car. The trees were moving, and the road – everything. My husband was away. All I wanted to do was to get back home as quickly as I could. You could see the water rising up over the reef, on into the harbour, and by the time I got back to Government House the lawns in front were two feet deep with water.

Then it slowly surged back, leaving all these fish and lobsters and crabs lying there gasping on the grass. Within minutes all the servants came rushing round to ask if they could go down and collect it. So they all got laundry baskets – anything they could – and came back laden. Later that evening they brought a lovely seafood selection for me and the children so that we could all be part of the feast.

Finally, the wives decided they'd come with their children out of their quarters, and sleep in the house with me. But we had to move out of Government House because we didn't know how badly it had been damaged. So we went into this large wooden building in the grounds that was a sort of office, because I knew from experience that a wooden house, even an old one, was safer than a stone one in earthquakes. The gardener got beds in for myself and my two small daughters. Everybody else brought their bunks or some mats and pillows and Gods knows what, and we had a lovely time. I got the women to sing because the children wouldn't go to sleep, of course. So there we were, with our hurricane lamps, all singing and telling stories until we fell asleep. It was great fun – the Fijians made it like that, they always did.

5
At Home with Queen Salote

In 1939, the young Ronald Garvey was dispatched to the independent Kingdom of Tonga. Her Majesty Queen Salote had been on the throne since the age of eighteen and was already something of a legend in her own country, where royal traditions had sacred roots going back to the tenth century. The treaty relationship between Tonga and Britain was an affectionate but tenuous affair, confined to advising on foreign policy and the establishment in the capital of a British agent and a British judge. In this particular case, Garvey's mission was far from straightforward.

I was sent down as quite a junior officer, only a fortnight before the outbreak of the Second World War, with instructions from my High Commissioner to interview Queen Salote and to persuade her that on this occasion the Tongans should declare war and join the Allies. It was felt that Tonga was a possible stepping stone in the Pacific for attacks on Fiji and perhaps New Zealand. Nobody was supposed to know that I was going there to ask the Queen this rather vital question. So I was given a kind of cover. I went ostensibly to look into a quarrel over status which had developed between the Agent and Consul, who was the British representative there, and His Honour the Chief Justice.

But this sort of minor diplomatic fracas was the least of my problems. What I had to do, which was far more important, was to try and find out something about the Queen's attitude towards the impending war. The question was, how could I get an introduction to her? In the end I found out that her private padre had an audience with the Queen every evening after evensong in the Royal Chapel. So I thought that he could soften the Queen up and then perhaps an audience could be arranged. In fact that was how it all worked out, and I was in due course summoned to the Palace.

For a Tongan, a visit to the Palace merely required the donning of the *ta'ovala*, the ceremonial waist-mat worn over the usual shirt and kilt. For a European, the correct dress was rather more demanding.

We were very formal in those days. I put on my striped trousers and morning coat and top hat, and went along to the Palace, this elegant white house on the edge of the sea, where I was greeted by a very courteous Tongan ADC who took me into what I call a salon. It was just like a gorgeous old-fashioned Victorian drawing-room. I can't say that the aspidistras were there, but almost everything else was. I sat down, feeling very distinctly nervous, when there was suddenly a sort of rustle and in came the Queen, a statuesque figure, six foot two inches to be precise – a lovely lady in every way. I stood up and made what I hoped was a court bow, and she said, 'Oh, Mr Garvey, do be seated. Do tell me how you're enjoying your visit to Tonga.'

Then she very sweetly edged me round to more serious conversation and I started to talk as instructed about the international situation and the possibility of Japanese aggression. After listening to me most carefully she said, 'Well, Mr Garvey, I fully appreciate your High Commissioner's view of this matter. My Parliament is now sitting. I shall see in due course that a message is sent to them indicating that it be my wish that, in the event of war, we should declare war and become joined with the Allies.' That was it.

The English overtones of the Tongan atmosphere were not confined to the Palace, with its lace antimacassars, china cabinets and family portraits framed in oak – the buffs and sepias of Victorian photography rendering the bearded princes in their pearl tie-pins indistinguishable from the European dignitaries. True, at Nuku'alofa market you could buy anything from a dried octopus to a braided girdle of female hair, and on the wharfside the fatted pigs from the outer islands disembarked with their owners from the little cutters and the copra boats. But elsewhere it was a town of flagstaffs and statues, bells and red-painted spires, with sudden 'English' vistas. The criss-cross lanes behind were overhung with cottage gardens, full of stocks and lobelias and pink and white roses. There were fretwork verandahs and picket fences, and painted shells lined the front porches, rainbow-coloured through patterned glass windows. Often it was as cool as an English spring, though almost always the sun was shining. Black umbrellas were raised against it, parasol style, and beneath them padded the graceful, slow-moving Tongan women, careful of their complexions wearing high-necked dresses, and long black skirts, their hair tucked up into plaited tiaras, their mat overskirts swathed round their hips like bustles. There was little traffic to disrupt this leisurely ripple of movement, for few Tongans owned a car, even in the capital.

Tongan traditions blended the best of both worlds, the European and the Polynesian. On special occasions, military parades and services of thanksgiving would be followed by ancient rituals such as the royal *kava* circle or the installation of a noble, solemnly staged against a backdrop of sun and sea. Any colonial officer appointed from Fiji to one of the few official posts in Tonga considered himself fortunate, even though the only regular communication with the outside world was the monthly steamer from New Zealand. The mail from England took six weeks *en route*, and there were no air services. But balanced against this isolation were the sheer beauty of the islands, a sense of history rare in the Pacific, and the well-known hospitality of the Tongans.

Another attraction was the undeniable romance of the Tongan royalty. Most British Consuls established firm friendships with Queen Salote, who had succeeded to the throne in 1918. The young J. S. Neill, who went out in 1927, was no exception, and he also became close to the Queen's husband, the Prince Consort. Official business was conducted over an informal bowl of *kava* at the Prince's morning visit to the Residency, and a light-hearted attitude was taken towards any paperwork involved. When, for instance, some vital documents were washed overboard from the royal canoe in a particularly high sea, the Prince reported the episode, 'breaking into loud laughter at the climax of the story'.

The Residency stood on the seafront a hundred yards from the Palace. It was a solid, rambling bungalow built in the early 1900s of New Zealand kauri wood, with the usual iron roof painted the national scarlet. The sole drawback was the plague of mosquitoes emanating from the narrow space between floor level and the ground beneath. The only solution was to have the building lifted several feet to enable air to circulate freely. A civil engineer from Fiji advised that such a thing was impossible without severe structural damage. But, as Neill described in his book, he then consulted a Tongan carpenter.

One morning without any warning my old Tongan arrived with about sixty men to do the job. I told him that, of course, he'd have to give us time to find other accommodation and to move furniture. He looked puzzled at this request, said there was no necessity to move anything and laughed at the idea of leaving the house. He then told me that he would brace the verandah with lengths of timber at regular intervals. All we needed was a ladder for getting in and out of the house while he was lifting it. Jacks were produced, and slowly inch by inch he raised the house to a height of about nine feet. When the jacks would go no higher, oil drums were used to give extra lift. Concrete posts were made for a new foundation, levels taken, and the house slowly let down and bolted into position. After that, a hurricane couldn't shift it. The Residency was six feet above ground level, and the only damage was a bent piece of mosquito gauze!

As a Judicial Commissioner, Neill had to deal with the kind of cases not often encountered in a British court – the settlement of hostilities between rival female supporters in a local football match, a fatal fire aboard a copra ship, and a slanderous feud between two white traders who both proved to be stone-deaf. He also found that the radical idea of a prison without bars was no new concept in Tonga. Up to the early 1900s, prisoners lived at home and reported daily for duty until they had 'paid up' their sentences at the rate of a shilling a day. Thirty years later, Tongan prison regulations still displayed the essential Polynesian attitude of *laissez-faire*, as Neil discovered.

One day I nearly drove over a prisoner who was asleep on a country road near a quarry where his gang was working. I wrote a note to the responsible Minister, a good friend of mine, pointing out the unfavourable impression that would have been created if I had been a tourist off the steamer from New Zealand. The Minister asked for details of time and location, and then replied that the prisoner was indeed asleep. But as this had occurred during his dinner-hour no regulation had been broken. This reply was conclusive!

Even in the 1940s, a colonial officer appointed to Tonga found himself playing a bewildering range of administrative roles, especially if, like John Brownlees, he was also a qualified lawyer.

I was an absolute Poo-Bah! I was Secretary to Government. I was sitting with the Cabinet and the Privy Council, and then I was also Acting Chief Justice. I seemed to be the person whom people came to see if they wanted something done. I was only thirty-one. Certainly I had no right to the judicial scarlet, or anything of the sort, in English eyes. But I was a barrister and I had brought out my counsel's dress – white wig, short black robe and so on. So, knowing the Tongan passion for ritual and tradition, I wore it quite blatantly on every occasion. I hope it impressed them – it was the best I could do.

On Sundays all things came to a stop except eating, sleeping and church-going. The constitution declared that 'The Sabbath Day shall be sacred in Tonga for ever and it shall not be lawful to do work or play games or trade on the Sabbath.'

It was no joke, this legal control of behaviour on a Sunday. It was very strictly observed indeed. Eventually I got over that by borrowing a horse from a white planter. I'd ride around his estate and then have a quiet swim. But there was no question of anything else. With the Tongans it was a national voluntary observance. It was in the law, of course, but it had become so customary to them that they never thought twice about it.

Some pastimes were frowned on whatever the day of the week. Any kind of dalliance, for instance, between European visitors and young Tongan women had to be conducted very discreetly indeed, lest public morality should be offended. The Queen herself kept a watchful eye on the daughters of the aristocracy and did not hesitate to intervene if a scandal was indicated, as occurred during John Brownlees' period of service in Tonga.

It was when the Mormon Church was trying to establish itself very strongly indeed. But they made a classic mistake. They sent young male missionaries, and some of them didn't last six months. The Queen would have a quiet word with someone and the young man would leave. Why they sent unattached young men, I do not know. Perhaps it was intended to be a test of their characters, but quite a number of them failed that test, and the Mormons never really got going in Tonga after that.

Charis Coode, arriving in Tonga with her husband James after twelve years in Fiji, received her first offical summons to the Palace with some trepidation.

Queen Salote asked me to go round and call on her. Having never been used to calling on queens, I didn't know how you would get out of the room at the end of a royal audience. Anyway, I went in and immediately forgot all my nerves. We had a very nice *tête-à-tête* tea, and when the time to go arrived I thought, 'Now what?' But the Queen got up and just took me by the arm, led me right out to the front entrance and actually put me in the car. She was so good at that kind of thing.

I got to know her well and I especially loved her sense of humour. When colonial officials came to visit us, the wives didn't always come with hats, and of course you don't go to the Palace without a hat and gloves. It wouldn't have done. So I used to keep a store of hats and fit them out accordingly, and the Queen told me later she had got to know my hats and she always amused herself trying to guess which hat was going to turn up next.

Returning the Queen's hospitality also had its problems. When Neill was Consul and Agent, he was startled to observe that one of the other guests at his dinner party, a noble called Ata, was consuming neither food nor drink. As a kind of Lord Chancellor, he was not allowed by Tongan custom to eat in the royal presence. Sympathetic remarks were made to him which the Queen, out of politeness, pretended not to hear.

Perhaps because of the complexities of the Tongan taboo system, it was thought safer to employ Indian servants at the Residency, though the Coodes' cook had idiosyncrasies of his own.

He was a marvellous cook. He was called Jackie, and he was nearly blind and totally deaf, so I used to write up any directions for him on a blackboard. But he was totally unpredictable.

When the Queen came, we had a rather grand dinner party. Just the day before the little Tongan boy next door had sent me a piece of his birthday cake, and on it was a rather chewed-looking pink celluloid angel with little wings. I'd sent this out to the kitchen and forgotten all about it. So we had this rather elaborate dinner and for a finale we had an ice pudding. Much to my astonishment, when this confection was brought in by the butler, perched on top of it was the pink celluloid angel with the wings. Queen Salote caught my eye, because she knew my cook, and burst into laughter.

Guests staying overnight at the Residency were in for other surprises.

We had a store room at the back of the house and the rats used to run round it quite happily. Well, we didn't mind too much. But unfortunately it was connected with the spare room, and of course the guests weren't awfully keen on this. Added to which we had some very horrible claret, and the rats had cottoned on to pulling the corks out of the bottles, so sometimes there was rather a row in the night. If we had anybody terribly important we used to put them in our room, which was on the other side of the house. But because the partitions between the rooms didn't always come up to the ceiling, the rats simply used to run along them and drunkenly sit and look at you. Some people would be horrified, but you got used to these things.

6
Another Pattern of Islands

The far-away Gilbert Islands were immortalised by Robert Louis Stevenson in the 1880s, when he and his family arrived as voluntary castaways on the island of Abemama, home of the Micronesian tyrant King Tembinok. In these isolated 'warrens of men ruled over with some rustic pomp', the impact of European civilisation was crude and sporadic, dependent largely on the efforts of one Hiram Bingham of the American Board of Foreign Missions, and the occasional drunken whaling crew. Stevenson summed up the South Seas as 'an extraordinary no-man's-land of all the ages . . . a stir-about of epochs and races, barbarisms and civilisations, virtues and crimes'. But it was left to a twentieth-century government officer to make this particular 'pattern of islands' a household name.

Arthur Grimble went out as a young cadet in 1914. He became a Gilbertese scholar, publishing learned ethnological papers. But it was not until the 1950s, with his broadcasts and his first, best-selling book, that he revealed himself as a *tusitala*, a teller of tales in Stevenson mould. These minute specks of coral became real and vivid to people in Britain 12,000 miles away.

Grimble dedicated *A Pattern of Islands* to 'the District Officers of the Colonial Administrative Service and their long-suffering wives'. But young newcomers such as Andrew Armstrong knew Grimble through a rather different publication in the 1920s.

Grimble had written a book called *Hints and Instructions to District Officers*, and we were all brought up on that. He was a charming person, very tall and thin and good-looking, and had a wonderful voice. He was a brilliant linguist and spoke Gilbertese as nobody has ever spoken it, I think.

Gilbertese is a strange and difficult language of only thirteen letters and a range of guttural sounds. Armstrong remembers hearing Grimble speak in public.

All the elders had come down from the villages and he

addressed them for twenty minutes in Gilbertese, non-stop. I couldn't understand a word of what he said, but I asked my clerk the next day what he talked about. And the clerk said, 'I don't know, sir, he was talking the language of the old men' – that is, classical Gilbertese.

Grimble was a pioneer in many ways, as his daughter Rosemary has pointed out, not least because he was one of the first administrators to see the islanders not simply as subject people, but as a people in their own right, with their own culture and traditions to preserve.

That was very important to him, very important indeed. They were people from whom he felt he always had so much to learn. To him, they were the higher chiefs, as it were, and he was the student. He was a gatherer. His papers say very little about himself, in fact nothing. It was old material gathered in Gilbertese that concerned him most. Often he would do his own translations into English. But people who really want to investigate the rest of the papers have to know Gilbertese. Above all, he loved meeting people and talking to them, and this could only be done in their own language.

Rosemary Grimble Seligman was born in the Gilbert Islands, the second of four children. No English child had been born before in Tarawa, the main island of the group, and great enthusiasm greeted her arrival. The Grimbles left for England only a few years later, in the early 1920s, but in that short time she had experienced an extraordinary introduction to life.

In Beru there was this beautiful house, which was specially made for my parents when they arrived on the island, because the person who was there before had left taking half the house with him, including the verandah. So they built an entirely new house which was done all out of local materials. There were no nails and all the beams were bound together in the Gilbertese way. I remember walking round wide verandahs, feeling the wind through the shutters, and the cool darkness, holding my nurse's hand. At night in bed you looked straight up at the rafters. They seemed so high up. Somehow the darkness always had light in it, and movement and sound. The palm trees outside, and the way the fronds would turn over and rattle in the wind, that's the sound I most remember. And then suddenly you'd hear a coconut falling on to the sand with just one thud, no more.

Strangely enough, though, I remember mostly a sense of anxiety, almost fear, although I was so young – perhaps it was because of our geographical situation, being out on the edge of the world. The land is so tiny, and the sea is so huge, and so is the sky.

All the Grimble children spoke Gilbertese as their first language, and never used English at all with their nurses.

We each had our own nurse, and we all used to play under the palm trees. We'd be told stories, and they'd show us how to make these cat's cradle things, string figures which have a tale to them. It's a very important part of their culture, the string figures. There's a canoe and there's a spear, and one or two others that I can still do, even now. As for clothes, I still have a photograph of myself in my little grass skirt, my *ridi*, which I kept for years. Or else we wore some strange shapeless garment like a suit of rompers – much too big.

Apart from tinned stuff we had a Gilbertese diet, often very limited. On some of the atolls there wasn't any fruit at all, but we had coconuts and coconut milk. I've grown up with a deep hatred of ordinary milk. I used to tell my parents it would make me sick, but this was held to be nonsense, especially by my grandparents. However, I learned later from my father that milk was referred to by the Gilbertese as a thing to make one vomit. My mother used to send away for these great tins of powdered milk, and the Gilbertese, at that time anyway, thought it was revolting and so did I.

The life of the villages also left its traces on the mind of an impressionable young child.

I remember walking through villages with my nurse, the little houses on stilts on each side, so neat, so beautifully kept, and the deep shadows across the pathway. One could see people passing through a palm grove in the distance and they always seemed to be moving slowly from light to shade, and there was always movement of sun across the leaves. The lane between the houses was quite wide, but not so wide that you coldn't talk to your neighbour opposite. To the Gilbertese, it was very bad manners to walk between two people talking to each other across the lane, and I still have this hesitation about walking between two people, even if they're standing on the pavement talking to each other.

Throughout Rosemary Grimble's life, the influences of the Pacific have remained strong. She has edited and published many of her father's papers, and as a professional artist her drawings and illustrations often reflect these South Sea sources. Much of her research concerns traditional magic – not surprisingly, considering the Gilbertese respect for the supernatural.

Everything was imbued with spirit, everything had its own ruling spirit. And so there would be magic that would affect it. You could put a spell on your palm tree to protect it from your enemies. Your cooking hearth was another thing you always had to protect very carefully, because of possible use by enemies. They might put a bad spell on it, so you'd have to be able to counter that with a different spell. There were spells for going out fishing so you'd get a good catch, and before a canoe was built the right place, near where a man slept, must first be found. For this, ancestral gods would be consulted. The place must be *mauri*, or blessed.

They also had their traditional medicines. When she was quite young, my elder sister Joan had beside her eye a vein which opened and bled profusely all the time. The European doctor couldn't stop the bleeding. Nobody could stop it. Then one of the Gilbertese came forward with a leaf or mixture of some kind which he said would cure it. My mother was rather reluctant about this, but she changed her mind because of a fright she had. One evening she went to the cot and she thought somebody had taken Joan away and put a Gilbertese baby there instead, because a dark-skinned child was lying in the cot. In fact, it was Joan's face covered with blood; the vein must have got worse. Then this Gilbertese came and applied the mixture to the vein, on the place near her eye, saying 'Now it will get better', and it did. It never opened again.

Inevitably, the time came for leave-takings. Grimble himself returned to the Pacific, but for the children life in that extraordinary island home was at an end.

I remember very clearly when we must have been leaving because there were at least two canoes, and they were piled high with luggage. Then we were in a big ship going to England and I was in a cabin staring up at a shelf above the bunks where there were some oranges. I climbed up, got them down, and my sister and I ate the lot, skin and everything. We'd never seen oranges before. We all caught measles on board, and I had a badly infected leg as well, so when we got to England I was carried ashore. It was winter and very cold, and apparently my first remark was, 'The trees have no clothes on.'

Following in Grimble's footsteps in the Gilberts was no easy task for a senior administrator, but Andrew Armstrong looks back now on his first years in the Gilberts as a comparatively carefree time.

The whole thing ran itself to a considerable extent. You see, you have a native magistrate and his court. Our job was simply to oversee proceedings. We'd never heard then of Parkinson's law, but Parkinson's law was operating even in those days. Somehow or other we imagined we were greatly overworked, terribly burdened. In point of fact we were doing nothing.

Even communicating complex events could turn out to be easier than expected.

I remember when Edward VIII abdicated, I sent for the old men to tell them the news. I thought it would make a tremendous impact on them to know that the King of England had given up his throne. They listened very attentively, and then one of them piped up and said, 'Ah, *tiani*!' which means 'woman', and that was that. After all, they had their wives and they had their divorces and so on. Adultery was one of the major sins. It was also an offence under the native laws, and when the laws were originally codified the punishment was imprisonment, though this was later rescinded. As far as they were concerned, this was a penalty that the King had to pay for his misbehaviour.

The most demanding aspect of a District Officer's duties in the Gilbert and Ellice group was the sea travel involved. The whole area covered two million square miles of water, though the total land surface was a minute fraction of this. At least ten of the Gilbertese islands had no interior lagoons. Passageways in through the reefs were navigable only by canoes or whale boats. Under abnormal sea or weather conditions communication became not just dangerous but impossible. But communication was the focal point of government, as James Coode points out.

Each island had its own little government and I had to get round them whenever I could just to check on the books and see the people. Almost all these islands were often very difficult to land at – huge waves and rock coral just beneath. But somehow or other we'd come ashore. Then I had to get them to break off some of the welcome ceremonies to manhandle the stores ashore, after which I would go to the little office and collect the stamp money, count the stamps and so on. This would have to stop every half hour, because they'd say, 'Excuse me, sir, the women's committee want to welcome you', and the women's committee was very important, of course. So I sat back while dancing went on, and little presents would be given – woven baskets, shell necklaces, half a dozen eggs – for about another half hour. Next the Village Improvements Society or the Choral Society wanted to welcome me, and more or less the same people would keep coming back all day. It was really delightful if you could just keep calm about it, and not worry about schedules or anything to do with time.

The greatest possible asset for a District Officer was to be good at sailing, or at least keen to learn. Given the expertise of the islanders, it wasn't long before a young cadet such as Andrew Armstrong became a veteran handler of the traditional outrigger craft.

They were wonderful canoeists, and their canoes were splendid pieces of construction, every plank held together by sinnet string from the coconut tree. Racing was the great sport. Of course, you can't travel for very long distances at full speed. When the wind blows, the *rama* – the outrigger – lifts and the crew runs out on to it, and that enables the hull to cut through the water with this enormous sail at tremendous speed. Then perhaps the wind lessens slightly, and the outrigger comes down into the water, and of course that takes the speed off immediately, and the crew comes back into the body of the boat. When we were in Tarawa I used to sail nearly every evening, going out after the office at about four o'clock. I would take a policeman with me, and a few prisoners from the jail, and out we'd go in a canoe, probably with another one standing off to race in the lagoon. Some of the prisoners sailed better than the policeman.

Equally at home in the sea were the Polynesian inhabitants of the Ellice Islands, where every family had its own canoe. Fishing was a way of life, a ritual performance with its own legends, initiation rites, poetry, and masters of ceremony – all echoes from a long-distant past when the ancestors made land after months of voyaging across the Pacific. Fishing parties were exciting occasions, as James Coode remembers.

Night fishing in the Ellice Islands was best of all. You went out in a fleet of dugout canoes, and to see the dawn come up over the horizon was something marvellous. They had a fishing rod at the back of each canoe, and if you were lucky enough to go through a school of bonito, they just seemed to swarm around you. If the hook was there, the fish would bite it. The natives used lighted flares of coconut leaf. The fish would come out of the water towards the light and everyone would make a dart with hand nets to catch them. It was extraordinarily exciting – and very eerie, too, because you'd see the reflections of other canoes here and there with their flares, and you'd be aware of the reef and the waves. I sometimes had a go but I didn't often catch anything. It could be a bit precarious and I just felt I was jolly lucky not to fall in. At the end, the bottom of the canoe was full of fish, and then when you got back in the middle of the morning, all the village were waiting on the beach to count the proceeds and share them out, singing to welcome us home.

Andrew Armstrong also took part in the fishing.

I spent weeks and weeks on the island of Nanumea, which is the most northerly island in the Ellice group and totally isolated, and I thoroughly enjoyed it. I remember I entered into one of the fishing festivals – offshore fishing with hand nets. I was in the water with some beautiful maiden holding my hand for about an hour. I got so cold I had to give her up, alas, and retire to my hut. But that was my only regret.

To be the only European on the island, or perhaps on a whole string of islands, could mean you were called upon to deal with all kinds of unforeseen emergencies, as Eric Bevington discovered.

I remember one night sitting on my verandah reading an out-of-date paper, the old kerosene lamp hissing overhead, when there was a knock on the door, and in came Tutu, the island medical practitioner, just out of training school.

He said, 'I've got a man in hospital, and he's got something blocking his intestines. I'm afraid I'm going to lose him. I think I ought to operate, but I daren't lose him on the operating table. Will you come and give the anaesthetic?'

I'd never done it before but I knew what the drill was, so I agreed. All I had was an old mask and a dropping bottle of chloroform. The technique was basic but effective: you dripped chloroform on the mask as the fellow lay on his back on the table. After a while you took the mask off and stuck your finger in his eye, and if there was any reaction you needed more chloroform. So you put some more on and then you lifted off the mask and stuck your finger in his eye again, and if there was no reaction you'd say, 'Go ahead.'

After this I helped Tutu several times at operations, and I think he rather liked to have me there.

Often wireless communication of a primitive kind was the only link between one island group and another. Naturally the arrival of the first commercial radio sets caused intense interest, as Andrew Armstrong remembers.

The islanders were extremely impressed with the beginnings of the BBC and reception from England and Australia and New Zealand. I was one of the pioneers with a wireless set and of course there were awful disasters. I would ask the native magistrate and some others from the village to come and listen to it. Then at the crucial moment the wretched thing would break down and they would laugh and say, 'Another thing of the Europeans that doesn't work!'

Innovations and new entertainments often arrived via the District Officer's wife. These were also a useful means of communication, as Charis Coode found when she was living in a Gilbertese settlement on the Fijian island of Rambe.

I couldn't speak Gilbertese and not many of them had much English, but I did start a knitting class. We also had Guides and Brownies. As the DO's wife I was OC of the company. We used to have quite a lot of fun, lighting bonfires and cooking things on campfires and so forth. They were also very useful for forming guards of honour if visitors came.

The cinema was just a hut with a tin roof, and whenever we could get hold of a film we'd have a show. Just before it was due to start, they would arrive at the house with little chaplets – garlands of flowers – one for me and one for my husband, usually made of frangipani or marigolds. They'd put these on our heads and then they'd pick up two chairs and, duly crowned, we'd march in front of the procession, down the hill to the cinema. We'd sit on our two thrones in the middle of this shed, with all the children at our feet. The Gilbertese had very definite tastes about films. They didn't like the love scenes. In fact they used to sit with their hands over their faces and peep through two fingers, and they didn't think it was very nice. But I remember them seeing *Mutiny on the Bounty*, which they really enjoyed. I think they'd heard about the story, and of course they loved the sea scenes because this was real life, and they spent all their lives in boats. Then after the film was over we would be escorted home again.

Every now and then, however remote the island, there was a first-class diversion by way of a viceregal visit. This event was greeted with enthusiasm by the islanders and apprehension on the part of the District Officers, especially if, like Eric Bevington, you were still on the very lowliest rung of the administrative ladder at the time.

I was a cadet in my first station, Beru Island in the Gilberts, and we heard that the High Commissioner, in other words the Governor of Fiji, was coming. Moreover, he would be staying one night with me and my new young wife. She, of course, was absolutely petrified. We also heard that the old boy liked to see native dances. As it happened, the local ladies were spectacular performers of the Gilbertese dance called the *ruoia*, wearing these very heavy grass skirts, but topless. The High Commissioner, Sir Harry Luke, was well known for having a great eye for beauty. When I got the message I was away from my headquarters on a ship. So I immediately sent a signal back to the only radio station on our island, which was the mission station. The message was to the senior native official, saying, 'Get the dancing girls ready. And make sure they're topless.' It was not at all well received by the missionaries!

The formal arrival of a Governor at one of his South Sea islands was always a highly picturesque affair. Traditionally His Excellency was carried ashore by stalwart islanders, enthroned on a bamboo litter and liberally draped with leaves and flowers and as many Union Jacks as could be found. Despite the charm of the welcoming ceremonies, though, Eric Bevington inevitably encountered the kind of misunderstanding familiar to all Pacific administrators.

We had talked to the natives about the Queen's representative as the most important of all men, and His Excellency had the good sense to come ashore in full uniform, with cocked hat and feathers, the lot. This was terribly impressive, but there was one drawback. He was a short little man and he had with him an

ADC who was about six foot three, a magnificent figure, and being an artillery officer he had one of those huge metal scabbarded swords that hang almost horizontal to the ground on chains. So the native community clearly thought that the big tall one was the Governor, and the little fellow was a sort of jester. Imagine trying to translate ADC into Gilbertese. However, we got around it by saying that the big fellow was a ceremonial guard of some kind, the keeper of the little man's body. The little man was the high chief and he had to have a big man to look after him because he was so powerful. This actually went down very well.

Fortunately there were no doubts about the effectiveness of the grand finale of the visit, planned for the end of the evening, even though there were a number of domestic hurdles to be surmounted first.

We had to entertain the Governor to dinner in a sort of tiny little box-bungalow. To start with he brought about six people with him. All we could afford was a single cook-boy, a servant from my bachelor days. We also had to contrive this meal on one of those dreadful old Dover stoves for which the only fuel was coconut husks notorious for their smoke, because wood was far too valuable to burn. So we hastily shanghai'd one of the police constables as a waiter. He'd never waited in his life before, and when he came tramping round with the vegetables it was obvious that they weren't properly boiled. In fact they were extremely hard. His Excellency nobly tried to cut a potato in half with a spoon and it cascaded sideways. I will always remember the look on my wife's face as the policeman's thumb came across and firmly anchored the potato, while His Excellency completed the operation.

After all that, we went on to a magnificent evening of dancing, the kind of thing that's absolutely non-stop with a terrific noise and crescendo of excitement. For the great dance, the *ruoia*, the men accompanying it clap steadily faster and faster and the women's hips have to keep time with the clapping, and the men go on clapping until the last woman to keep time is left in, and she is the winner. The old boy certainly showed his appreciation of this. And the people, as they always do, immediately picked up his enthusiasm and they went to town and gave us a terrific night, a really magnificent show such as only the Gilbertese can produce. When I think of the South Seas now, that's the picture that comes to my mind, and always will.

7
Palm Tree Justice

For raw recruits to the Pacific in the pre-war years, the British Solomon Islands Protectorate provided a harsh antidote to any illusions of a lotus-eating way of life. It was not only a poor colony, it could also be a dangerous one. Blackbirding, the kidnapping of islanders for plantation labour, had been stamped out but otherwise the Pax Britannica, was still only skin-deep, as superficial as the narrow fringe of coastal settlements that lay scattered beneath the mountains and forests of the huge double chain of volcanic islands. This was Melanesia, the South Seas of the *Boy's Own Paper* – traditional home of cannibals and head-hunters, where cool-thinking, bush-hatted Englishmen defended themselves and the friendly natives against the spears and arrows of enemy tribes.

There was no shortage of real-life examples. Eric Muspratt, a young adventurer who went out as a planter in 1920, wrote of Tulagi, the principal port and seat of government, as

> only slightly civilised. There was an old-fashioned gallows not far from the hotel, and just before my arrival it had been in action. A white trader named Laycock had been killed with an axe. The government had captured six natives who were concerned in it and condemned them to be hanged. Not a sign of fear was shown by these six boys. They stepped proudly and importantly up to the platform, grinning at their friends and apparently delighted by the sensation they were causing. So, casually and playfully, they died, one by one.

About the same time, an old Pacific hand called J. Macmillan Brown reported that, on his visit to Malaita in the east of the group, 'A Mr Daniels, of Miss Young's Queensland Mission, was shot when conducting service; a chief had offered 350 fathoms of shell money – i.e. about £90 – for a white man's head, it mattered not whose. The murderers are still undiscovered.'

More relevant to the cadets was the episode always cryptically referred to as the Bell and Lillies affair. William Robert Bell was a District Officer in Malaita, a solitary, idealistic man with twelve years' experience of patrols into the interior, on foot and by canoe, and many a bı ush with head-hunting chiefs. In 1927, Bell and a young cadet named Lillies set off into the jungle to collect taxes, gather in unlicensed firearms, and initiate a programme of village sanitation.

Taxes proved the sparking point. Only the year before there had been fierce protests by angry villagers, led by one Basiana. Despite this, once they reached the collection area Bell and Lillies took their seats at two tables in the jungle clearing, alone apart from two policemen and a clerk. To avoid provocation, Bell had ordered his escort of armed constables to wait inside the tax house behind. The tribesmen filed forward in two lines from the back, and within minutes Bell was dead, struck on the head by Basiana's rifle as he bent over the table. It was the signal for a massacre. Lillies, the clerk and twelve constables were speared and chopped to death before a shot could be fired. Two constables escaped back to the ship, and the culprits fled. A punitive expedition was mounted with a bungling lack of success, and it finally took a search party of Solomon Island police to bring the murderers to justice. Basiana and five others were tried and hanged, and several more were given life sentences.

This may have been of some slight reassurance to Ronald Garvey when, as a Colonial Service cadet, he found himself following in the footsteps of Bell and Lillies just a year later.

One of my first jobs was to set out along the coast to Sinarango to collect hut tax from the same tribe that had killed my predecessors. But I had a posse of police, the Armed Constabulary, they were called, and it was their duty to look after me while I went through the essential process of collecting the tax. The tribespeople had to come along to a kind of clearing where there was a native rest house. Then one by one they came forward, gave their name, and put down their five shillings. I gave them a receipt, and off they went for another year. But in view of what had happened, I did devise a new procedure of my own. In order to protect myself I had the police in a V coming down towards my table, with the natives coming in single file down the centre. And then at the back I had another V of police to prevent anybody coming from behind to obliterate me like they had poor Bell and Lillies. It seemed to work well and I stuck to it thereafter.

As a qualified magistrate, John Brownlees found that in remote areas the people often set the machinery of justice working in their own special way.

More than once the people themselves had captured someone who had offended against not only native law and custom but also our own criminal code which was based on it. They always brought them in in the same way – what they called 'long pig'. They'd get a stout stick and tie the man's ankles together and his wrists together, and he was carried in like that, with his head lolling back, just as their ancestors had brought in the dead of their tribal enemies whose bodies were to be cooked and eaten. These prisoners could easily have been made to walk, but it was to humiliate them that they were carried in like this – and, of course, it must have been very painful.

On tour, you had to be prepared to hold court wherever necessary. It might be in the middle of a path under the shade of a large banana leaf, at other times in a rest house in a rain-soaked mountain village. Sorting out the exact nature of the wrongdoing was no simple task.

You relied on your fundamental sense of justice. But you sat alone – there was no representation on either side – and the whole village would come in and listen. And don't forget it was done in pidgin English, so nine times out of ten the accused didn't understand a word of what was going on.

Pidgin English was supposed to be the lingua franca of Melanesia, where there were so many native languages that tribes living within a few miles of one another might be unable to communicate with each other. However, since it originated from Chinese traders – 'pidgin' comes from the Chinese word for business – many tribes found it hard to master. So did the English administrators who had to pass examinations in it. For the administration of justice, pidgin was not the most accurate of instruments.

John Brownlees sometimes found it difficult to be impartial, especially surrounded by truculent, near-naked bushmen when local feeling was running high.

I was always influenced to a certain extent, wrongly or rightly, by the audience. Their reactions to the proceedings were not put into so many words, but they were highly expressive: 'Waaahhh!' would mean 'You dirty liar!'. This was often very helpful, and certainly did influence you. Above all, you had a strong sense of trying to get to the root of the matter, and seeing fair play. There was no finesse or nonsense about admissible evidence. That kind of thing never crossed my mind.

For Ronald Garvey, this system had a certain pragmatic virtue.

You were the Magistrate but you were also the Prosecutor because you were the Chief of Police. You were also the Superintendent of Prisons to see that the accused were looked after, if you sentenced them. But you were able to do it all in an extremely impartial way. In Malaita most of the crimes in those days concerned adultery. It sounds odd to think it was a criminal offence, but in the Solomon Islands of those days adultery was regarded by the native people as a crime, and so we had to accept that. If the adultery was proved, and it wasn't usually very difficult to do that, the stock sentence was three months, which was very useful. It was a South Seas tradition that prisoners should help out with a variety of outside duties. I'd keep the prison full with three-month jail sentences, so my gardens and station were extremely well looked-after. Most of the prisoners were very happy to serve a little time on the government station. Discipline wasn't very strict, they got good food in the prison, and we all got on very well.

In fact, it was the custom in some places for ex-prisoners to refer to their jail sentences as time spent 'in the government service'. But not all government ideas were so amiably received. Taxation, for example, was something John Brownlees himself considered basically unfair.

Whereas we Europeans were not taxed, be we government or planters or commercial people in stores and so on, the natives were. There was a poll tax, and it varied from island to island. Some bureaucrat had said, 'Oh well, Gizo in the north, they're more missionised, therefore they must be better off.' So they had a pound to pay, which was a lot of money in those days. Malaita was only five shillings.

But what was even more unfair was the dog tax. You were exempt from the head tax when you were sixty. So a chap would get all his friends round saying they remembered old Jimmy, he was born eighty years ago, this sort of thing. Well, how could we know? If we were in a good mood we'd accept it, if we were in a bad mood, we wouldn't. So when it came to the dogs, they'd try the same thing. But there was no exception for dogs of any age.

In those days the territory had to pay its own way; there was no subsidy from England at all. The only exports were copra and trochus shell, and if the market was bad, there were no funds. As Dick Horton points out, 'You couldn't educate people properly. There were only two doctors in the whole place. I don't know how we would have managed without some very good native medical officers trained in Fiji.'

Malaria was widespread, as was TB, and there were frequent epidemics of dysentery, measles and whooping cough. But the worst scourge was yaws, which infected its victims with sores and ulcers that ate away at limbs, face and head. For this disease regular injections were the only cure, and Nick Waddell remembers one man in particular who had dedicated himself to the task.

There were two kinds of injection. One was a lead compound and the other an arsenic compound. The cures were quite remarkable, miraculous really, and people would come from far and wide, particularly to get the arsenic kind, which gave you a bit of a pickup, as well as curing your yaws.

To carry out this work the government employed the very remarkable Gordon White. He was a bluff, red-faced chap from the Australian outback, and he travelled on his own all round the Solomons, at times for weeks on end, never seeing another European, injecting the populace with these drugs. He was a very popular man and a very tender man, too. He loved what he was doing, and he loved the people – this was his work in life. But he did like his jug of ale.

Once I was visiting round the coast and came to a house which belonged to a famous planter called F. M. Campbell. There was nobody living in it at that time, and Campbell permitted anyone who was travelling in those parts to stop over there, if they needed. So I rolled in on a canoe early one morning and went up to the house and there was Gordon. He was sitting with no shirt on, a bottle of beer or two by his side, staring at the sea, looking completely terrified.

I asked him what on earth was the matter.

'The sea,' he said. 'First it's coming in, then it's going out, then it's coming in again, and I've only been sitting here since breakfast.'

Poor chap, he was convinced he was having an attack of DTs. Thank goodness, I was able to reassure him, as I'd seen the same thing myself more than once. What had happened was there had been an underwater explosion. We had a lot of earthquakes on the island, some of them out at sea, and this had affected the tide, making it recede and come up again several times within the space of an hour or two. And here was Gordon, goggle-eyed at his glass of beer, desperately wondering if it was too late to join the temperance movement.

For a white man working alone in these remote corners of Melanesia, the long periods of isolation could prove a test of domestic management, as John Brownlees recalls.

There was an Australian firm called Mackleross – they were the Sainsbury's of Sydney – and you ordered all your food from them. It only came once every six weeks to Tulagi, and of course in the out-stations you only got it every three months. So you had to plan well in advance whenever it was time for the order to go down. Our great fear was that the onions and potatoes would be put in the same crate and one or the other would always go rotten, which was a disaster.

Nick Waddell was also a faithful Mackleross customer. He discovered that, without wifely advice, there were certain pitfalls in the system.

I made a great mistake once, because I was rather partial to ground rice pudding and blancmanges and that sort of thing, and I remember my mother always used to grate nutmeg on top of them. So I was looking down the catalogue one day and saw nutmeg. I had no idea how much to order, and so I thought, well, seven pounds should be enough. In due course I opened the crate and took out bag after bag of nutmeg, enough to last for twenty years or more. I daresay the Japanese got it in the end.

Books brought out from England tended to fall victim to silverfish, white ants and other print-devouring insects. So once again, as John Brownlees recalls, you turned to the ever-helpful Mackleross.

They would get library books for you. You joined a subscription library and got sixteen books at a time. I always remember one which impressed me tremendously – *Lice and their History*. It was an enthralling tome of 800 pages: the effect that rats, the carriers, and lice themselves had had on the human race, the plagues they'd brought, and so on. I was absolutely intrigued by it and read it several times. Not exactly romantic. One couldn't afford to be. It would be too disturbing mentally to read romance sitting alone over one's whisky. There was certainly no romance in the Solomons, believe me.

The romance may have been lacking, but not suspense. There were real-life ghost stories in plenty. All through the South Pacific, the District Commissioner's house was a favourite site for a haunting and the Solomons were no exception.

At Kirakira, the headquarters of Eastern District in the Solomons, the District Commissioner's house was said to be frequented by the spirit of a young girl who haunted lonely bachelors. The story was that around the end of the eighteenth century this island girl, who was famous for her beauty, bestowed her favours on no fewer than eight young men. But the ninth she resisted, and by way of revenge he employed a sorcerer against her. The spell was successful and she died, since when she had haunted the huge tree that had been her meeting place with her lovers. Eventually the tree was cut down, and the house built on the same spot. Apparently the young lady found it just as congenial for her various activities – especially the verandah, as Guy Wallington relates.

One District Commissioner used to sit out there at night, looking out to sea or reading a book. It was an L-shaped verandah, and round the corner was a table with a bowl containing ping-pong balls. Suddenly, round the corner, a ball came rolling and bouncing down towards him. He just picked it up, put it back and then started reading again. Then another ball came down, so he did the same again. It happened a third time, and by this time he was a bit fed up. So he picked the bowl up and locked it in the bedroom. 'That's enough for tonight,' he said, in his best DC's voice, and wasn't disturbed again.

Others had the same sort of experience: doors opening, for instance – those mosquito screen doors. Not banging in the wind or anything. But a door would open just before anyone went through it. After a while they got in the habit of saying 'Thank you very much,' and simply going in.

Then it was my turn to live there. I can remember sitting having a solitary meal in the dining-room, and feeling a distinct tap on the shoulder the very first night. I turned, but there was no one there. I was willing to put the other things down to the fact that the floor was a bit uneven. The whole house was on stilts, and it might have sloped a little. But there's one thing I just couldn't account for. That night when I was sleeping in the bedroom there was a sudden drop in temperature, the kind of

Trader named Nielson on the verandah of his Florida Island store in the central Solomons, c. 1890 (courtesy Royal Commonwealth Society)

Above: *Missionary Lloyd Francis on a visit to a Melanesian hill village, c. 1930 (courtesy Revd D. Lloyd Francis)*

Above right: *Ronald Garvey, guarded by armed police, collecting taxes on Malaita in the Solomons, 1928 (courtesy Sir Ronald Garvey)*

Below right: *Arthur Grimble at the Residency on Ocean Island in the Gilberts, 1929 (courtesy Andrew Armstrong)*

*Andrew Armstrong with his clerk on Butaritari Island in the northern
Gilberts, 1930 (courtesy Andrew Armstrong)*

Philip Snow and the Vanuabalavu cricket team at Lomaloma ground, Fiji, 1940 (courtesy Philip Snow)

Bearded Choiseul Island coast-watchers (Nick Waddell right, C. W. Seton centre) with American sailors during the war in the Solomons (courtesy Sir Alexander Waddell)

Above: *Patient arriving for medical treatment at Ysabel Island in the Solomons, c. 1946 (courtesy Christine Woods)*

Right: *Queen Salote entertaining Queen Elizabeth and Prince Philip at a traditional Tongan feast during their royal tour, 1953 (Popperfoto)*

Governor Sir Ronald Garvey being served a ceremonial cup of yanggona *at Queen Victoria School, Fiji, 1953 (courtesy Sir Ronald Garvey)*

James Coode with Prime Minister Tupou (son of Queen Salote and later King of Tonga) at the opening of a new wharf at Niuatoputapu, Tonga, 1963 (courtesy James Coode)

thing you never get in that climate – a terrific wave of cold. My first reaction was to pull the bedclothes over my head. I thought, 'Gosh, it must go away. This is awful.' Well, after a bit, the temperature seemed to rise a bit and I chucked the bedclothes off. I said, 'I know it's you. You're there all right.' I burst into the bathroom, but there was nothing, nothing at all. I never saw her, but I felt her presence.

Dick Horton was startled by another echo of the pagan past when he was on Malaita in 1938.

I really met the last cannibal in the islands. I was going across country up in the high bush, and there was this old man wandering about. I asked him in pidgin what he was doing.
  He said, 'Oh, I'm looking for a body to eat.'
  So I said, 'What kind of body?'
  'Oh, any body,' he said.
  I said, 'What part do you like best?'
  'The thumbs,' he said.

Sometimes a whole village or tribe would revert to pagan beliefs, and a District Officer had to be both tactful and ingenious in order to preserve the peace. Horton was woken one night to be told there was trouble in the village of Vololo on Guadalcanal. After a series of births of deformed children the people believed that a spirit shrine on the mountain top must have been violated. Arriving on the scene, Horton suggested a performance of one of the old sacrificial dances to appease the god. At once, the pigs were brought down from the villages for the feast.

It was amazing to see the change of atmosphere from one of fear and dread to cheerfulness and laughter. A crowd of a thousand gathered. The moon came up and fires were lit and the pigs were roasted. It was unforgettable. The dances came from the edge of time. The music was made by pan pipes, nose flutes, wooden drums and the stamping of feet. It was clear that everyone was happy and I went to bed.

Jack London wrote of the Solomons, 'Murder stalked abroad in the land, and the air seemed filled with poison.' This Melanesian quality of menace seemed particularly real when you lived, as John Brownlees did, in one of the wild hill stations among a people still basically governed by their old tribal passions and beliefs.

It was a very beautiful station and the house was well above the police lines and the prison. There was a village about half a mile away, but my place was about 200 feet up and out of sight. So at night one was completely isolated. There was the jungle just behind and that was all. Sometimes I'd go out fishing in the government vessel, or wander down and chat to the villagers. But I must confess that late at night everything seemed different. It didn't help that you got malaria fairly frequently. I had it seven times in the Solomons. Feeling ill, you'd get rather frightened. If you heard a noise or a rustling in the bush, you'd start imagining all sorts of things. When you're passing sentence on people, it means you're always living as an outsider, you see. It's a tradition, so you certainly got a little nervy at times. I decided once to get myself a dog. I got one, but not for long. He was definitely poisoned.

It was little wonder that the borderline between reality and imagination could become blurred on some occasions. Nick Waddell remembers one example.

It was New Year's Eve, and being a Scotsman I was a bit sentimental about this, and I had helped myself to a glass of something. I wasn't exactly celebrating, though – I was working on my annual report. There was no typist, no clerk, nothing like that on the station. You had to do all your own work and typing was one of the great hazards, because everything smudges in the heat, the pages stick together and so on. I was in the little box I had as a study, typing away by the light of a kerosene lamp – an Aladdin lamp they called it – which gave out a white, eerie light and made a sort of hissing noise. Suddenly, above the sound of the lamp and the typing, there came from nowhere the music of bagpipes. As I say, I'd had only one glass of whisky. I thought this could only be my imagination. I must be cracking up at last. And then in the corner, I noticed my old wireless set that hadn't been working for months. I'd obviously left it switched on and something had happened to make the battery go again. So here were the bagpipes coming from Scotland, bringing in the New Year. After that the poor old machine expired and died, but it had been a famous last minute.

8
The Thin White Line

However involved the British administrators became with the lives of the islanders, they were still, inevitably, the outsiders, strangers in the midst of those close-knit Melanesian communities with their private dramas of family, village and tribe. Out on a lonely station, a government officer could sometimes feel curiously irrelevant to the world around him. At moments like this, most expatriates would experience not so much homesickness as a simple longing for the company of their own people, that thin white line of fellow Europeans scattered throughout the huge distances of jungle and sea between one settlement and the next. Nick Waddell remembers his nearest neighbour, the local planter, on his outpost at Makira in the southern Solomons.

In the evening I'd walk along to Campbell's place for a drink, and then back again. That was a good four miles each way and I felt I'd earned my drink. Sometimes I stayed for supper with him. He would recite the Australian poets, Banjo Patterson and the rest, by the hour, and the sight of this huge, gaunt man declaiming in the lamplight with just myself for an audience – it was quite something. He was such great fun to be with.

In emergencies, too, there was no better neighbour than a practical-minded planter, as Robert Lever discovered.

A particular case that I remember was putting my jaw out. The effect of this is that you have to keep your mouth open and you dribble the whole time. Fortunately for me there was a planter within about half a mile, so I wrote on a piece of paper, 'Have dislocated my jaw' – because of course you can't speak at all. I got a towel to hold over my mouth, and rushed over to this man. He was an Australian, and fortunately he had had experience with stock. He simply got himself in the right position and shoved his thumbs into my mouth, having first covered them with his handkerchief so that he didn't get bitten. It worked right away.

As a magistrate in the Solomons, John Brownlees would regularly go on circuit among the outlying islands, visiting each plantation in turn.

The routine was always the same. You landed, the manager was waiting there, he greeted you, and then the labour force was lined up. 'Any complaints?' you would ask them. Usually there were quite a number of complaints ... abuse by the master, not being fed properly, and being overworked. Theft amongst each other was another problem. I held a very informal court session, often in an old copra shed.

Then traditionally, that done, the manager would invite one to share the evening meal – it was something to look forward to. But their wives were the saddest creatures I ever met, very pleasant people basically, but so lonely. Their husbands would be out on the plantations all day, or up at the nearest settlement. But the wives were tied to their houses, completely isolated, and this sometimes made them rather difficult to deal with. In my experience the husbands very seldom commented or objected to one's decision about labour troubles. But then the wife would say, 'What did Mr Brownlees do about Lasu who attacked you?'

'Well, he found him not guilty,' or 'He discharged him with a caution,' might be the reply. The look of fury that crossed the female's face didn't lead to a very happy atmosphere for the rest of the evening.

There was the other side of the coin, too. The labourers might naturally be thinking, 'What justice can I get from a man who listens to me, and then half an hour later I see him sitting on the master's verandah sipping whisky?' Mind you, it was usually my whisky.

For a professional entomologist such as Robert Lever, the Solomons' great, gloomy rain forests concealed unexpected treasures. Although the major part of an entomologist's work was the eradication of pests – the bugs and beetles that destroyed the coconut crops, malaria-carrying mosquitoes and others – the hunt for rare species of wildlife was always a compelling interest. Toads and fruit bats were commonplace, as were the beautiful birds of the Solomons – the frigate bird, the white-necked kingfisher herons, and the bright green parrots of the jungles. But when Robert Lever came across something unusual he had to work quickly to put it on record.

You always had to pin up your specimens in the evening of the day you had collected them because obviously they deteriorated. This meant working right into the night after dinner. It paid to be friendly with the Medical Department, because they were able to let you have spirit for preserving. Once I had a most interesting lizard which I was keen to get to London. But I had no fluid except whisky, the last inch in the bottle, very precious. But I gave up my evening tot in the cause of science and off it went. I only hope the people at the other end appreciated what a sacrifice I'd made.

Of all the creatures of Melanesia, the most valued, apart from the ubiquitous pig, was the turtle. The shark was worshipped by some clans as the embodiment of the ancestral god, as was the porpoise. But all over the Pacific the turtle shell was a market commodity, and the meat was the food of chiefs. This meant it was the natural choice for a presentation ceremony when an important government official arrived. Unfortunately for the soft-hearted British, the traditional method of presentation was to keep the turtle on its back, still alive, before its throat was formally slit by the welcoming party. Even then there were fresh ordeals to come, as Guy Wallington recalls, on the visit of a new High Commissioner.

After the ceremony we were all sitting on the top deck when we saw a dinghy arriving. In it was a bucket with what looked like loads of ping-pong balls. The High Commissioner looked over the side and said in a jolly way, 'What's all this?'

They said, 'Oh, they're turtle eggs, a hundred and fifty of them. They've been brought for Your Excellency because they're a delicacy.'

Well, that night we had dinner on the top deck, and all the smells from the galley wafting over us were of turtle cooking. Having had that for an hour or so, it was time to dine . . . turtle soup, followed by turtle steaks, with turtle eggs as a savoury. At which His Excellency said, 'I've had enough,' and disappeared. After that, none of us ever wanted to see a turtle again, dead or alive.

The Solomons' own head of government was the Resident Commissioner, whose headquarters were at Tulagi, the main port and settlement of the group. The whole island of Tulagi measured only about three miles from end to end, and Dick Horton found he could inspect its main buildings in less than an hour. Such a small community had its own social eccentricities.

I'd not been in Tulagi for very long when I was invited up to dinner by the local doctor. In those days we had to be very pukka – black tie, black cummerbund, long mosquito boots and all the rest of it. Afterwards he suggested we had coffee outside on the lawn, and he told his boy to bring it. No coffee turned up, so he called him again. 'Simeon, where is fella coffee?' And he answered, 'Oh master, me sorry too much, arse piece belong coffee pot im e bugger-up finis.'

This shook me rigid. I thought, 'Good lord, does he really use this language to his master?' But all he had said was, 'I'm very sorry, the bottom of the coffee pot has burnt out.'

Dick Horton also found the Tulagi golf course unlike any other.

As it had been made out of swamp, it was extremely difficult to play. From the first to the second hole you had to go over a ridge and the ball would land in the sand. Your little piccanin would run round to make sure that the crabs hadn't pinched the ball and disappeared with it down a crab-hole. Then the last hole was a tremendous biff into the wind, and the ball would swing out over the reef and they'd have to go and dive to get it.

Some rather more exotic games had also been invented to while away the evenings. One in particular Horton still remembers.

You get some bottles of beer and put them in a bucket of water. That helps to cool the beer down and it also loosens the labels. So when you take the bottle out, you detach the label and stick it back inside out. Then the idea was to send the bottles of beer spinning upwards onto the ceiling, and if you hit it lucky the label came off on the ceiling, facing downwards. Then the bottle was yours. A friend of mine was very experienced at this game, but I am afraid when I played it I stayed thirsty most of the night.

There was at least a doctor on the station and island medical practitioners throughout the districts. But a dentist was almost unheard of, according to Dick Horton.

We used to get a wandering dentist of somewhat bibulous character, who came up to the islands about once every two or three years from Australia, but I never ventured into his grasp. One day, though, I was crossing a river in a canoe with my headman, Soniluvu, miles from anywhere. I had a screwed-in tooth, and as I leaned over the side to see how deep the water was the thing dropped out and disappeared without trace. In a place like the Solomons that tooth was invaluable. I just had to get it back. So we turned the canoe and spent ages peering down into the water. Suddenly Soniluvu spotted it – a tiny gleam of white at the bottom – and without a thought of crocodiles I dived in and grabbed it up out of the mud, got back in the canoe and we went round to my district station at Aola. Eroni Leauli, the Fijian medical practitioner, stuck a piece of gutta-percha into the hole – sterilised it first – and rammed the tooth back in. There it stayed for five years until it dropped out in the rather different setting of the Barbizon Plaza Hotel in New York.

Europeans who found conditions primitive in the Solomons had further readjustments to make if they were posted on to the neighbouring New Hebrides, a tangled archipelago of almost a hundred islands rising up from coral reefs to jungle peaks and smoking volcanoes of four thousand feet or more. Hurricanes and tidal waves competed with earthquakes, and the annual rainfall sometimes reached 200 inches.

The government had made little impact on the Stone Age way of life of the inhabitants, which made the islands very attractive to anthropologists and biologists such as the brilliant young Tom Harrisson, who went out with the Oxford University Expedition of 1933 and 'went native', as he put it, for a year among the tribes of north-west Malekula.

The British operated on an official power-sharing basis with the French in the New Hebrides, an arrangement which cut across all the usual colonial patterns in the Pacific. The Governor of Fiji declared it 'a remarkable and absolutely new experiment in the joint, yet separate administration of two great Powers in one area' when he sailed down to declare it open in 1906. The influential Presbyterians, however, were against it from the start. The title of one of their early pamphlets, 'Under Two Flags: a Hopeless Experiment and a Grave Scandal', summed up what most people felt about the Condominium, as it was called. Inevitably, it was rechristened the Pandemonium.

In the red-tape jungle of duplicated rules and regulations, each at odds with the other, the *entente* was rarely *cordiale*. There were two sets of coins and postage stamps, two separate medical services, two administrations in which every official was twinned on the other side. Each of the island group's four districts was in the joint charge of a British and French District Officer, whose totally different outlook on colonial policy made their combined operations extremely uncomfortable affairs.

This incompatibility was at its worst in the joint court. John Brownlees, sharing the bench with his French counterpart in the 1930s, found that they were poles apart in their attitudes to the cases brought before them.

Time and time again, we would agree on a verdict. Then it was a question of sentence. If I thought a sentence of one year's imprisonment was adequate, I would start with six months. He would immediately have thought two years, because they were so much stricter on sentencing in France anyway. We occasionally differed so much that we would have to go away and come back next day. Usually they were quite trivial offences. Many French planters imported Tonkinese labour and had a very bad reputation for severity. You can imagine a Tonkinese man, brought well over a thousand miles from a poverty-stricken country and signed on for two years. Unless he got some support he was in a helpless condition. The French officials obviously thought that I was just soft. They'd say, 'Look, there'll be a rising one day unless you're firm with these people.' My reply was, 'I certainly appreciate that Europeans who have to work with indentured labour have problems. But I cannot agree that firmness, as you call it, produces the right results.'

The legal situation was made more complex by the fact that British and French subjects carried their own laws with them, and each national administration possessed its own legal machinery to deal with this. In effect, if a Frenchman was fined he simply appealed to his Resident Commissioner, who more often than not would pardon him on the spot. It seemed that mutual understanding was hampered at every level.

There were three jails, for instance. There were two police forces. There were three public works: the condominium public works, the British public works and the French public works. Also the French colonial system itself had two distinct advantages, to anyone in it anyway. First of all they were seconded from the French Metropolitan Service, so they had a job to go back to on retirement, whereas our Colonial Service was a completely separate system. If you retired at fifty, there was no warm welcome for you in the Home Office. Secondly, and this was quite amazing, their salaries were metropolitan-based. The further away from France one was, the better off one was, so all their administrators were much better paid than ours.

It was hardly an arrangement to encourage good working relations.

There was tremendous rivalry – and there's no other word – between the two Resident Commissioners, the respective administrative heads, and it went right the way down to every District Office and District Officer. On a small station, their houses were next to one another. They were supposed to go on tour together, sharing the same boat, but they tried to avoid that. As for the social life, you could sum it up with the fact that we served beer, while the French popped champagne.

Sometimes, however, individual administrators such as Keith Woodward could laugh at the lunatic diplomatic logic of their situation.

My French counterpart rang up one morning and said, 'We've shifted our flag-pole.' Their Residency used to be at the same distance above sea level as the British Residency. Now they were about to fly the flag at the new French Residency, which was on a higher level. In fact it was overlooking our paddock, the British paddock. 'We're wondering if this is all right with you,' he said. 'We hope that you won't mind.' I thought this was terribly funny, terribly redolent of the old attitude in the Condominium, having everything equal and making sure that no one had any precedence over anybody else.

I said, 'Of course not. It doesn't matter in the slightest.' In fact I had no authority for saying any such thing. But I thought it was just too ridiculous, the idea of one Residency worrying about its flagpole being on a higher level than the other.

9
Spells and Miracles

'One night I had a dream. I dreamed of our Lord. You know that picture in St Paul's Cathedral of Holman Hunt's *Behold I knock at the door*? I had that vision, and I was determined to go . . .' These could be the words of any one of the nineteenth-century evangelical missionaries who responded to the 'Call to the Islands' with such visionary fervour. In fact they come from the Reverend Lloyd Francis, who went out as a young lay missionary with the Anglican Melanesian Mission in 1926.

'When I got out to the Solomons, I wasn't sure what exactly I was going to do. But when I saw the amount of sickness and disease, I thought, that's it!' It was 500 miles from his isolated mission station to the capital, Tulagi, and the nearest hospital. There was no wireless, no telephone, and the mission ship called only twice a year to deliver mail and foodstuffs. 'Then we were left to it.'

One of the major diseases was leprosy, and the most pressing problem was to make contact with the victims and then keep them in quarantine. Francis began going up into the hills in Malaita 'looking for lepers'. He organised a tiny settlement of four houses, one for the men, one for the women, and two for married couples. One old man called Batista was so badly stricken that he had no feeling left in any part of his body and his feet were reduced to stumps. So Francis built him a little hut of his own, with the special privilege of a fire where the old man could cook his yams and sweet potatoes. 'I used to look after him, go and see him every morning, take him his food and so on.' Then one night there was an accident with the fire. Without realising it, Batista had rolled on to the hot embers and burned a large hole in his buttocks. 'I had to tell him, "Sorry, no more fire, Batista." I won't tell you what he called me! I was quite shocked! I went on looking after him, poor old boy, and he died of nephritis in the end.'

There were other echoes of biblical times when not just the lepers, but the possessed, too, were brought to the mission house.

They brought me a madman once, a young fellow called Bebla, only about nineteen years of age and as strong as a lion. He'd been working on a coconut plantation but had been sent home because he was useless. So the natives brought him to me to be cured. I didn't know what to do, to be quite honest. So I let him sleep in my house. Then one morning he was missing. When I got back into my house, he'd taken everything off my breakfast table and put all sorts of strange things on instead. I didn't worry too much about that. Then I went into the cookhouse to chop some wood for the store. I didn't hear a sound until a rope went round my neck. I looked round and said, 'Bebla, what are you doing?'

He was laughing. 'Me catchem one chicken,' he said.

You see, if the natives wanted a fowl they set a trap, a noose, and when the rooster came to collect his food they would get him round the neck. Well, this time I was the chicken. I slipped out of that all right, but if I had acted too quickly I might not be talking to you now.

On another occasion, the situation was even more dangerous.

When I went in the cookhouse another day, there he was with the axe. I said, 'Bebla, give me the axe.' He stood up and raised it above his head to strike me. All the natives were crowding round the door to see what I was going to do. And I just repeated the same words. 'Bebla, put it down, put it down, put it down.' Gradually he brought down the axe and laid it on the ground. But if I'd have gone for him to grab it, he could have cut me down there and then.

About the same time that Lloyd Francis was dealing with the realities of mission life in the bush country of Malaita, another young man was introducing the rising generation to some of the basic principles of the English public school system. R. C. Rudgard was posted to one of the best-known Anglican establishments in the islands, All Hallows School at Pawa on the island of Ugi. It was 1922 and some of his pupils were not much younger than he was. They came from remote villages and islands that were often hundreds of miles distant, and their background was completely pagan. 'There were some who told me that their fathers had given them human flesh to eat. And then I found that my gardener, the old man who did my garden, was reputed to have eaten his sister when he was a young man. He certainly killed her. I know that.'

Christine Woods came up against pagan custom as soon as she arrived, as a nurse of twenty-one.

> I had a cook and she told me she had helped to kill her aunt, to strangle her. Actually she had held the woman down, while two other members of the family strangled her. The rule was then that if a man and a woman had misbehaved, the relatives of both sides simply took over. They went out with them into the bush, and they never came back again. No questions asked. The couple were killed and buried. That was their standard of morality when I went out there in 1934.

Christine Woods was to dedicate the whole of her working life to the Melanesian mission. At one time she had resolved to become a nun but was told she was not sufficiently 'good'. So it was as a lay missionary that she first went out to the islands that were to be her home for more than forty years.

> There was a long sea journey and we didn't arrive until night. Everything seemed very dark and very eerie. The children were there to see us come ashore – all these little black figures lined up on the beach staring at me with their huge, gleaming eyes. I was greeted by the headmistress and taken up to the school where they gave me some sort of stew. The vegetables, I remember, were boiled paw-paw and a kind of brown cabbage, which was really hibiscus leaves. I loved it all. I knew from the moment I arrived that this was absolutely the right thing for me.

Before long she was summoned to help with the kind of case that cropped up time and again in the Melanesian islands. To an outsider, it defied all rational explanation. To the local people it was the inevitable result of a particularly powerful spell against which there was no possible resistance.

> She was a schoolgirl of about eleven, I suppose, a very nice little child, and her temperature was up to 105 degrees when I was called in to her. Otherwise there was no symptom of any identifiable medical condition. I stayed with that girl, and prayed with her, but she was convinced she was going to die at sunset.
> 'Sister,' she said, 'you need not pray. I shall die when the sun goes down.'
> I couldn't do a thing about it. She died when the sun went down. It's terror, terror of the power of sorcery.

In the Solomons the most sinister of all forms of black magic was that practised by the mysterious Vele man as punishment for breaking some tribal taboo.

He'd get hold of a piece of bone belonging to somebody, and he'd put it in his little bag of tricks. There might be a finger belonging to somebody inside it too, or a certain coral stone, or a piece of bamboo – all sorts of things. But once a person had been shown the bag, sure enough that person would die. I always felt so helpless, absolutely useless, because their belief was so very strong. They could draw you a picture of the Vele, a figure with very long arms and very big feet and a very skinny body, and a pointed sort of triangle of a face.

To the islanders, he was simply an anonymous messenger of death. Often enough the victim would lose consciousness. Rarely would any European be able to break through this state of self-hypnosis, though one old planter is on record as bringing a young man round with a recitation of Genesis and a large dose of brandy.

The attack always took place at dusk, or later, and always well away from the village. The victim was held fast from behind, an incantation was uttered and the Vele bag was produced. Sometimes poisonous material was crammed down his throat, an element mentioned by the Right Reverend Derek Rawcliffe, who began teaching in the Solomons in the 1940s.

He would make a noise in the bush at night, a kind of hooting like a bird which always calls in the evening. We heard this sometimes at the school and the boys would say, 'Oh, there's the Vele man out,' and they'd be really frightened. They knew he wouldn't come into the school, but they wouldn't go out in the bush when he was about. One of the schoolboys told me that he had once been attacked by the Vele man and had lived to tell the tale. I believe that hypnotism came into it. He would say to the boy, 'You will go back to the village, you won't be able to remember who I am, but you'll know that you're going to die in so many days.' And so they would go back to the village, and they wouldn't remember, and more often than not they would die. This schoolboy also said that he had been saved because he had vomited. What I believe the Vele man does is to make people eat whatever it is he's got in his bag and it's this that kills them. When I was there, the government took this very seriously and it was a serious crime even to pretend to be a Vele man, but I don't think they ever caught anyone.

Strangely enough, the Solomon islanders' preoccupation with

sorcery and pagan spirits was a powerful factor in their progress towards conversion. As Christine Woods remembers, 'It was really easy for them to believe in our God, an invisible God, because their gods were all invisible.'

Jesus, on the other hand, was a flesh-and-blood reality. The Bible had been printed in the common language of Mota and, as R. C. Rudgard found, the parables and the New Testament miracles made a particularly powerful impact on a people whose whole culture was based on stories and the spoken word. Rudgard remembers being on tour with two of his pupils who had themselves become mission workers.

It was a certain village in Guadalcanal where the chief was a very noted heathen and he was a bit bolshie about this new-fangled religion of Christianity. The chief had gathered all his people together and was threatening to kill these two new Christians. Then suddenly the chief shrank back as if something extraordinary had happened, and he said, 'There were you two brothers, now there's a third.' Jesus coming to witness, you see. He was so impressed, he said, 'If your God you're talking about can come and stand by you, and appear like that, he must be somebody to hear about.' And of course they gradually became Christian.

These moments of revelation provided a vital spark of encouragement. Indeed, faith healing seemed the only possibility with some of the medical emergencies that faced Lloyd Francis. The case of seven-year-old Joe, the son of a local chief, seemed particularly desperate and the only possible diagnosis was tetanus.

His jaw was completely locked. He could eat nothing and he was having these terrible spasms in which the whole body became rigid. They would come on periodically, and the only thing I could do was to dissolve a morphia tablet and inject it into him, to give him a little peace of mind and comfort. The only way I could feed him was with soup through the spout of my teapot.

But I had so many sick people to look after on the main island that I had to tell the parents that the only thing we could do was to commend him into the hands of the Almighty: let Him heal the child if He can. We had prayers in the chapel, and I departed. I got back to my station of Yangamuli, and two or three weeks had gone by when a canoe came from Matima. Of course, the first thing I wanted to know was, 'What about little Joe?'

'Oh, he's fine. Fully recovered.'

Well, if that wasn't a miracle I don't know what was.

The islanders themselves often failed to appreciate the serious-ness of a medical emergency. Christine Woods, for example, had spent three hours as the guest of the local chief before she was told there was anything wrong in the house.

I was just leaving when he said, 'Oh, Sister, before you go, I'd like you to have a look at my grandson.'

I went in and found the child having convulsions, at the rate of eighteen a minute. He was two years old and I was horrified. I said, 'Pita, how long has this been going on?'

'All night,' he said. So I said, 'And you let me have lunch with you without telling me?' But that was Melanesia, you see. By now the father was walking about, saying, 'If my child dies I'll commit suicide.'

So I said, 'Suppose you go and say a few prayers instead of talking like that – you're no use to anybody. There's only one thing I can do,' I went on, and that is to try and get into the spinal fluid and relieve it. I've never done it before, and I haven't got a proper lumbar needle, only a large injection needle. But if you pray, God will help me, take my hand and do the job for me. Now go on, off you go!'

I knew that the doctor always put the patient round into a ball, so that the spine is well stretched. I did this, and I said a little prayer myself. I put that needle in, and it went straight into the spinal cord. I had to let it out very carefully because if you let it out too quickly the child can die – that much I did know. I took about a dram off first, and immediately the convulsions stopped. Those experiences were wonderful.

Even a qualified doctor at a mission station headquarters would find his hands full. Allenson Rutter was trained in tropical medi-cine but he was also a Fellow of the Royal College of Surgeons in Edinburgh, the first surgeon ever to serve in the Solomons. He was appointed medical superintendent of the Helena Goldie Hospital in the north-western part of the group and went out in 1938 with his wife Elizabeth, who had been working as a microbio-logist in a hospital laboratory. The operations he performed in these early days, in primitive conditions and with the minimum of equipment, were milestones in mission history.

I well remember the very first cataract I ever did. He was quite an old man by the time I operated on him and he hadn't been able to see for many years. When I was ready to start, Elizabeth very kindly got the book and stood at the head of the table and more or less told me how to do it, because I had literally never done one before. We bandaged his eyes and sent him back to the ward. The old fellow put up with the pain and the darkness, and in due course we took off his bandages.

Suddenly he cried out, 'I can see . . . I can see! Men like trees.' There's a Bible story about Christ curing a blind man, who says, 'I see men as trees walking.' This old chap was steeped in the Bible, and those were his first words.

Elizabeth Rutter has her own memories of her husband's operations. There was the man who was brought in trussed to a pole like a pig. Polio had crippled him up so that his arms and legs were permanently curled up like a baby's. The villagers called him the Crab Man, because for twenty years all he could do was shuffle around in the dirt.

Allen had special splints made in the workshop. You turned a screw and the tendons and muscles were stretched a bit each day. It took eighteen months and then came the day when he was able to walk like a tin soldier. His joints had lost their use, so his legs were rigid, but he could walk upright and that was a tremendous thing. His whole self-respect was restored.

Then there was the small boy known as Batwing. He had been so badly scalded that the scar had sealed his forearm to his upper arm. After a long, slow process of plastic surgery and skin grafting, the Rutters took him back to his village. The grin on his face as he walked ashore with his arms behind his back was the best reward of all.

To the island people, these were pure miracles. Allen was the first surgeon that they had ever had and they reached the point when to them anything was possible. They'd come with something that couldn't be coped with and he'd say, 'Well, you know, we can do no more.'

But they'd say, 'Just put me to sleep, doctor, just look inside,' as though you were unzipping a banana and by opening you up all could be cured. It was so hard to tell them that there were limitations even to the white man's skill.

More serious were the limitations imposed by a Pacific-wide shortage of funds. The Melanesian mission began training nurses in 1928 and, as Christine Woods recalls, the most useful asset of all was ingenuity. 'We were so poor when we started this hospital that we had no proper instruments or equipment. We used to cut bamboo and split the cane to make forceps. Bamboo, fortunately, is the most wonderful, useful thing under the sun.'

Sometimes local taboos caused unexpected problems. Christine Woods had once arranged for her Melanesian male assistant to attend to a woman who was haemorrhaging after the latest of a long line of births. He went into the house and was giving his patient an iron injection when the husband returned. 'The next thing, I heard a terrible commotion and found him beating up his poor wife because she'd allowed the male doctor to attend her. So I got another stick and said, "Unless you stop, you're going to get this cracked across your head." He did stop, but he held that against me for years. I never did it again.'

It seemed that Lloyd Francis, however, could do no wrong. Even in cases of childbirth, usually an event strictly taboo to men, he was the one to whom the villagers turned when things went wrong.

James, the headman, came to tell me his wife had given birth. He seemed to want me to go and see her right away. I went along and crawled into the hut.

It was full of women and smoke. I couldn't see a thing. But I could hear the voice of the mother and she was obviously in great pain. I gradually moved forward and I found her at the back, squatting and hanging on to a rope in the usual way they give birth. The child was alongside her, lying on a filthy coconut mat. I knew from my little book that I had to tie the cord and sever it. Well, this I did. It also said that you must wait for the placenta. So I waited.

Francis went on waiting from eight in the morning until one o'clock, occasionally massaging the woman's stomach, but nothing happened. Eventually he remembered his stethoscope and found his suspicions confirmed – a twin was still to come. The woman meanwhile was becoming exhausted.

I thought, 'She can't go on like this.' So I decided to make an internal examination, and what I found was that one arm was through, but it was blocking the head and the rest of the body. Well, I'd never had any training. I hadn't even got a pair of rubber gloves – nothing, no instruments whatever. The only thing to do was to ask the Almighty for guidance. So I just walked a few yards down to the village chapel, and there I put my case before the Almighty. And I *was* guided, because something told me that for that child to be born I must push the arm back into the uterus and get hold of the head, and that if I heated up some olive oil so that it would be reasonably antiseptic, this would make it easy for my hand to go into the uterus. And that's what I did.

I got the woman to lie down. Then I put my foot against one of the house posts and pushed the other way. Fortunately there was a fair bit of strength in me, and gradually I managed to get the arm back into the uterus, and then I felt around, grabbed hold of the head, brought it forward and the baby was born. When they saw it, they said, 'Oh, dead-finish.' But I detected a little bit of life, so I grabbed its legs and gave it a couple of whacks on the back and it started to cry. Well, of course, they'd never seen anything like that – nor had I.

10
Spreading the Word

The vital link between lonely outposts was a mission ship large enough to take passengers and cargo across the Pacific from one island group to another. But on a smaller scale, every mission station had its own launch or canoe, however primitive, and a large part of a missionary's life was spent scrambling in and out of these shaky vessels amidst the surf and surging currents of an island landing. As Lloyd Francis remembers, there could be moments of pure delight.

> We used to make the journey from one island to another in this outrigger canoe of mine. Once, about halfway across, a huge shoal of porpoises appeared. They were so close to us I could have put my hand out and touched them. It was a real joy to see them leaping up and down alongside us. They'd obviously decided to keep us company, and when we got near to the coast they disappeared. But I always remember that lovely experience of these marvellous creatures acting as our escorts all the way to the island.

In 1926, one of Francis' first postings was to the remote Santa Cruz islands, where the southernmost dot of all was a tiny atoll called Tikopia. Here the people were Polynesians, a handsome, exuberant lot who loved to trade on the rare occasions when a mission schooner paid a visit. Stick tobacco was the greatest prize and for this the islanders would barter their mats, baskets or anything else that was available. On this occasion, however, the chief who led the welcome party aboard came empty-handed. Alas, he had nothing prepared to offer, he said. But eyeing the tall young Englishman, he had another suggestion to make. His very pretty wife was one of the party. There below was the empty cabin. If the missionary would care to avail himself of her charms, say for half a dozen sticks of tobacco? 'Alas, I had to decline. After all, I did have my Bishop on board. And when I told His Lorship about it later, all he said was that in all the years

83

he'd been travelling the islands, no one had ever made him an offer like that!'

Travel by outrigger canoe in the island style presented a different kind of challenge. In her early days Christine Woods was blissfully unaware of the risks involved.

Sister and myself were sitting back to back on the platform affair that's lashed onto the side of the canoe. The boat was only a small one, and about a mile out to sea we were caught by a sudden squall. There was nothing to do but let this thing take us even further out to sea. How we stayed on I don't know. Our feet were dangling in the water all the time and we felt we were going to be pulled off at any minute. Finally we couldn't see any land at all. But those Melanesians really could navigate. Just at dusk, when the tide turned, we started to come back in again and the lads brought us safely home. We got in about nine o'clock that night, and we'd been out since midday. But do you know, the thought of sharks never entered our heads. Otherwise I don't think we could have held out.

It could take a full day and a half to get from the central Solomons to the eastern part of the group, where Mavis Salt was first posted to teach at a girls' school at Alanguala. On the mission launch, a cabin was a luxury and a lavatory non-existent. But the problem was solved when the Bishop presented her with a bucket and the Archdeacon held up a blanket. Soon after her arrival, she and a mission nurse called Jean were invited to join them on a visit to San Cristobal, an island notorious for its difficult landing. As usual, the last few yards over the reef had to be made in a dinghy.

There was a very rough sea. The surf was coming in but the boys weren't handling the boat properly. One minute we were sitting talking in the dinghy, and the next we were under the water. The thing had just capsized. It turned out that Jean couldn't swim at all and neither could the Archdeacon, although he'd been there so many years. Then the Bishop started panicking, and the reason was that he'd lost his false teeth. Then Jean called out, 'Never mind your teeth, Bishop, swim.'

Once ashore, the Bishop was still worried about his teeth. In such an isolated part of the world a replacement set could take months to arrange. Besides, he was due to attend a government meeting at the capital and was understandably reluctant to appear without his smile.

But a little bit later a dentist came down from New Guinea, a member of a rival denomination, and he made him a new set. Apparently his last words to the Bishop were, 'You might preach Anglican doctrine, Bishop, but never forget that you're doing it with Methodist teeth.'

The phrase 'daylight Christians' was a familiar one among all the missionaries working in the Gilberts, including the Catholic sisters, who could tell many a tale of *te anti*, the ghosts who were as real to the islanders as the coconut palms outside their doors. The missions often had to deal with cases of possession, for instance, such as one in particular of a young boy with his body distorted, screaming out in languages unknown to him, mixtures of Latin and French – speaking in tongues. In fact, the Gilbertese name for Lucifer or the Devil is *Neve-ni-Kabane*, which means Tongue-of-All.

But in the dazzling light of day, along the neatly swept veran- dahs of the mission station, the pagan past retreated. For a District Officer such as Kelvin Nicholson, the Catholic mission was some- thing of a haven, and there was always a special welcome from the priests.

They were marvellous people, and it was always fascinating to meet and talk to them. But what was also so delightful from my angle was that you could always get a first-class meal there. More important, they'd always seem to have home-brew on. If they didn't have home-brew, you were served up something equally good to drink. I remember once when the Resident Commissioner and his wife were touring with me, we called on the Catholic priest and the Sisters brought along a midday drink. It turned out to be tumblers of heavy Communion wine. You try knocking back a glass of that at midday with the temperature round about 90 degrees!

Younger priests might present a different image, dashing from one island village to another on a dusty motorbike, wearing patched trousers and shirt, greeted by teasing cries from the young girls who never undersood how a man could choose to live alone. Such a priest could turn his hand to anything, as Anne Sopper remembers.

I was travelling round the islands as a Field Officer for the Red Cross and when I arrived at one particular station I asked the DO's wife, 'Is there anywhere here I can get my hair cut?'
And she said, 'Oh yes, Father Meece, the Catholic priest.'

I said, 'Don't be funny – I really mean it.'

'So do I,' she said.

He lived in a little bungalow next to the church, and he had a notice outside his door, 'If your hair's not becoming to you, then you ought to be coming to me!'

Education, even of a primitive kind, was almost entirely conducted on the initiative of the missionaries. Right up till the end of the Second World War the British government had no schools of its own in the Solomons Protectorate, and all education work was in the hands of the five missionary societies, who were responsible for the various expenses.

Because of the huge distances involved and the difficulties of transport, most secondary schools were boarding establishments. When Mavis Salt became a headmistress in the northern New Hebrides in the 1950s, education for girls was still widely suspected by village people. They wanted to keep their daughters at home, waiting to be offered in marriage, but slowly the girls took things into their own hands.

They were all ages and very often big ones, too. They came to school when they realised it was useful to learn to read and write. Their parents didn't send them. The way they would do it was to make some copra, because this was the only way they could get money, by working at drying the coconut flesh. When they got enough to cover school fees, which I think were £1 a year – and a bit over to buy themselves a towel for bathing or something, then they would turn up and get some education.

Learning English was the first priority. Along with the reading and writing went some simple arithmetical tables, sewing, cooking and singing. Because they hadn't had the village schooling that boys were accustomed to, everything began at Class One and progress was slow.

The boys, on the other hand, had been initiated into the mysteries of the British boarding school system since the early 1900s. R. C. Rudgard realised this as soon as he went out as a teacher, fresh from Radley and St Augustine's College, Canterbury.

They were very good at picking up games, and they were especially fond of cricket. I remember we had a final of a house match and my side were losing. Then I happened to hit a ball which went right up to the top of a tree. You could see the ball up there, so when they shouted 'Lost ball!' I said, 'No, it's not a lost ball, there it is.' They couldn't climb this tree, so off they rushed to find some steps and then went up and got it. I made thirty-two runs and we won the match. Priceless, it was! My boys loved that.

Other Western novelties were not always so well received.

I introduced the first horse on my island, and the boys had only seen one in newspapers, magazines and so on. I shall never forget their reaction as it came ashore – the boys were so scared they climbed to the top of the nearest coconuts until it was safely landed and put in a paddock. And only two of the islanders wanted to learn to ride it – my batman and my groom. The others wanted nothing to do with it.

The basic structure of rules and regulations was something else many of the boys found difficult to accept. At his school in the New Hebrides, Derek Rawcliffe soon found that in Melanesia the relationship of teacher and pupil was fraught with difficulties.

You could never completely know them. You thought you did, but then there'd be some reaction which was quite strange. For example, I gave a bad report to a boy. This chap had been a complete nuisance all the time, and he was due to leave when the ship came. But he just started playing up worse than ever. So I asked him why he was doing this and he said, 'Well, it's what you wrote on that report. You said that I was a troublemaker, and so if I don't make trouble that report is a lie.' He was serious – he wasn't just being cheeky. He had to live up to what I'd written.

At all the island schools the daily routine started with the dawn. By midday it would be too hot for classroom lessons, and later on there was work of a different kind to be done. But discipline was strict, and when Mavis Salt's girls got their early-morning call they knew there was no lying in bed.

At half-past five the sell went, the hooting sound of a conch shell. Somebody had to get up and blow it. Then they would all go down to the sea for their daily bath. If you'd forgotten your towel it didn't really matter. You just dried off in the air as you came up again. Then each girl would get out her wooden comb – different islands had different patterns – and they'd spend about ten minutes doing their hair, which was very thick and curly and needed a lot of dressing. And then they were ready for morning prayers, so into church we'd go.

Every school grew its own food and often kept cattle for meat. When it came to a feast day, the girls themselves did the slaughtering, skinning and butchering. Lunch was green bananas, thrown into a forty-four gallon drum of hot water and cooked during morning school. Every girl had her own 'beach house' and her own bush garden, and in the afternoons they would enjoy their time off here, eating sugarcane, paw-paws and fresh pineapples, climbing for coconuts, or wandering out on the reef to catch fish and crabs. Then it was time to work again, at the most time-consuming task of all – cutting the grass by hand, with thirty girls in a row going over the sports field armed with the broad island knives that looked like pirate cutlasses.

They also sewed their own uniforms. They were maroon cotton, fairly practical, just skirts to start with because they were not used to wearing anything on top in the villages. Then one of the older boys who'd been sent to secondary school in New Zealand came back to teach in our school and he didn't approve. And so we had matching triangles made for Sunday best and then gradually, class by class, they started wearing them in school.

One of the main problems for a headmistress of a girls' school was her obligation to keep her charges out of the way of admiring males. A close watch had to be kept on all young men arriving in the neighbourhood.

Men came into the bay working on ships – they weren't very far away, just half a mile over the hill. But they had to ask permission to go off the station, and we would soon get to know if some of them came over at night. It would soon be passed on to you. Someone would come down and say, 'It's men coming.' And later on we had a dog and it always barked at men; it wouldn't bark at women. It even barked at the Bishop, and went for his trousers!

Segregation was particularly important because most of the girls were betrothed. Marriages were arranged between the two families when the children were very young indeed. 'It was the strangest thing', recalled Mavis Salt, 'to hear a little twelve-year-old say, "My husband's come to see me." It simply meant she was betrothed to him.'

Many of these social customs remained intact despite the mission influence. But inevitably the missionaries were the fore-runners of change. Some, including Lloyd Francis, had their doubts about the impact of Western ways on a people who had lived so long cut off from contact with the outside world. 'They loved to follow the white man and copy the white man. That perhaps was one of the tragedies of later years. They wanted everything the white man had, they tried to possess them, and I rather fear they became altogether too materialistic.'

One inheritance from the white men that could certainly not be described as materialistic was the reality of the Christian message. But in the final analysis, many would say that the most valuable legacy of the missionaries was the gift of education. The island schools, perched on remote headlands or deep in the forests of the interior, opened doors for the young generation in a way that fifty years earlier would have seemed impossible. As Rudgard remembers, 'Many of them were so impressed by school that they trained to be teachers as soon as they could. Quite a few of my boys became priests and two of them were eventually made bishops. After my retirement, I went out again to represent the Church of England at their enthronement ceremonies, and I felt so proud.'

But the impact of one culture upon another, in Rudgard's experience, was a two-sided affair.

I became so native-minded, I felt completely one of them. They taught me so much about my own religion, too. To them, Chistianity was a complete new way of life, something that mustn't ever be spoiled, and when they took a thing up they took it up properly, with no half-measures. I'm still very, very thankful to them for the years I spent with them. I've missed them so much since – more than I can say.

II
Coconut Kingdoms

In the popular imagination, the typical white man in the South Seas is neither the missionary nor the government officer, but the beachcomber – a romantic adventurer who has found the island of his dreams and a lotus-eating way of life to go with it. The image includes a gentle island wife at his side, a brood of laughing bronze-coloured children, and a thatched home surrounded by the waving palms of a flourishing copra plantation.

There were some who fit this picture, at least in part. 'Charlie the Londoner' had blackbirded for the Queensland sugar planters before acquiring a rich piece of foreshore through his native wife, paying off his debts with his copra profits, and achieving a 'quiver-full' of thirteen children. An Australian whaler was converted to mission teaching, and 'Mountain George' remained a lifelong hermit except when sickness drove him down to the European settlement where he could obtain the three essentials of life – newspapers, tobacco and salt.

But there were more stable elements among the settler population – craftsmen and storekeepers, pensioned-off administrators and retired skippers. Above all there were the planters – not the managers employed by the great companies such as Burns Philp and Lever (known as 'The Octopus'), but the private estate-owners, small and large, many of whom were second- and third-generation descendants of the pioneer families of the mid-nineteenth century.

Outstanding among these were the Hennings brothers, who, in their heyday, were said to own two-thirds of Fiji. Apart from their cotton plantations, they also ran trade stores and shipping lines throughout the islands, and even set up a national bank whose notes were known as 'Hennings Shin-Plasters'.

Young William Hennings set the seal on the family fortunes by marrying a Fijian woman of royal blood called Andi Mere, or Lady Mary. Daughter of the legendary war chief Ratu Mara and famous throughout the islands for her beauty and intelligence, Andi Mere lived on into the 1920s. To her small granddaughter Sophia Hennings she seemed a rather formidable old personage, still living in the style of a Fijian lady of rank in a traditional house which her son had built for her overlooking the sea.

She used to sit there outside, and when my elder sister and I used to go fishing we always had to pass her house on the way back. She'd say, 'What have you got in your basket?' So we'd have to show what we'd caught, if anything. Then she'd pick one out and eat it raw, there and then. It rather shook us, I must say.

A succession of violent hurricanes and the collapse of the South Sea cotton market in the 1870s brought the family to the verge of ruin. When Sophia's father Gus took over, the estate had been reduced to a mere half dozen islands. Brought up on one of these idyllic outposts, she remembers a way of life that was unique.

Looking back on it, I suppose it was rather abnormal really. We were going through a very bleak period financially, and we wanted to dive for pearls. But my father said, 'No, you have to do something useful. If you bring up enough clams, you might find a few pearls as well.' The clams were those great big things, very heavy. Then we did find one beautiful pearl shell, an enormous thing. We spread newspaper all round it so that if anything was spat out, it wouldn't be lost. But after all that there was nothing in it at all – terrific blow to all our marvellous plans!

One day, they found a cave which had obviously been used in the old days as a place of retreat from invaders. It could only be reached by ancient steps constructed by the islanders. Nearby was another cave containing human bones, including a complete skeleton. Sophia and her sister took home the skull as a trophy.

We put it out on the verandah, and for the next few days none of the local people would come near the house. There was no one to make the beds, do the sweeping, or anything else. So I asked my old Tongan nurse, who knew everything, what was the matter. She said it was the skull. They were scared to death of it and the whole place was *tambu* until we took it back to the cave. So that's what we had to do.

The girls were taught by their mother, who had come out to the islands from Germany. It was considered very important that they should be brought up in the old European style as far as possible. But there was no getting away from the daily grind of running a copra plantation and, as there were no sons, Sophia in particular soon got used to working alongside her father.

He and I used to get up at four o'clock in the morning. Then at five o'clock he would go down and beat the old wooden *lali* drum, and that would summon the labour force. We'd have breakfast round about seven, after which my father would retire to the office.

We always had to be keeping a weather eye open for showers. The coconut was spread out on reed trays to dry, and it mustn't get wet. So if a black cloud came over, there were always a couple of boys on the homestead ready to rush around and cover it all with corrugated iron. Knowing the Fiji climate, it probably didn't rain at all and everything had to be uncovered again.

Then about midday, either he or I would go up to the plantation in a lorry, which was the only vehicle on the island, of course. We had to collect the first load of copra and bring that down to be dried. And then there would probably be two more trips during the afternoon. Three hundredweight a day they had to make. If they could make more, that was overtime, and they got a shilling a hundredweight for that. Sometimes it was six o'clock before we finished.

Then you would go back to the house, have a shower and dress for dinner – long dresses, mark you, and quite a formal dinner. Afterwards one of us might play the grand piano – my father's special pride – or else read on the porch.

Sometimes there were trips to neighbouring islands in the Lau group, or to the main island of Viti Levu, which was two or three days' sailing away. The inevitable day came when the launch broke down. To their horror Sophia, her sister Liz, her father and two of the plantation boys began drifting away from the Fiji group altogether. The last blob of land was the lighthouse island of Wailangilala, and thanks to her father's navigational skills they got through the reef and into the lagoon. Wading ashore, they learned later that the waters were infested with barracuda sharks and that they had been lucky to make land at all – not that there was much of a welcome awaiting them.

There was only the lighthouse keeper, who was a cured leper, and an Indian with his wife and family, who was there merely in case the lighthouse keeper should fall ill. They were practically out of food anyway. The government yacht was supposed to call in every three months and drop supplies, but it hadn't called. All we had were a few biscuits, but we lived mainly on pumpkin tops. There were pumpkins growing all over that island, and mixed with coconut milk they weren't too bad. We lived on that for about three weeks.

It seems extraordinary, but neither the keeper nor his assistant had a dinghy or boat of any kind to go fishing. The theory was, I suppose, that they might leave the island altogether and the lamp would not be lit. Eventually a sailing boat turned up with a skipper on it whom we knew. Word had got round in the usual way that we were missing, although there was no radio and nobody had any contact with anybody else at all. But this skipper had just sat down and worked out that we were going from here to there, the wind was in that direction, and we must be, if we were anywhere, on Wailangilala – which we were.

In their late teens the beautiful Hennings sisters began to grow restless at the lack of social life in the remote Lau islands. Shipping called rarely and other European company was non-existent. Not surprisingly, a visit to the colony's capital was a great event, with wardrobes planned and improvised long in advance.

Once a year we would go to Suva, Liz and I, and we would stay at Government House, which was marvellous because Murchie Fletcher was Governor at the time, and he was very good to us. We'd usually time it so that there was either a German cruiser in or the New Zealand fleet, and loads of parties were held. I remember once there was a Fijian ceremony of welcome for the Duke of Gloucester, and my sister and I were there in our traditional regalia as descendants of the Thakombau family, and he very sweetly asked us how many words of English we knew. Then, after three weeks, we had to go home again.

After a few years, we decided this was not much catch really, so we started saving our pennies. We received the princely salary of £2 10s a month from my father for helping him on the plantation, and we decided to save that and go to England.

When my father saw that we were really in earnest he said, 'All right, you can draw on an endowment fund which I've started for you.' So out of that we paid our passage and came to England.

Closer to the centre of the group, the planters' paradise was the island of Taveuni, known as the Garden of Fiji. Here prosperous settler families lived in a feudal style with echoes of the Raj. Their huge, rambling bungalows were crammed with an exotic mixture of the Victorian and the Polynesian.

At teatime visiting ladies in hats and gloves were waited on by Indian bearers, in starched white uniforms and cummerbunds in the family colour, who handed round silver trays of China tea and cucumber sandwiches, or thin bread and butter with the home-made guava jelly that was obligatory in every well-run island household. Not far away, beyond the rolling gardens of bougainvillaea and hibiscus, there would always be the sickly-sweet smell of coconut, and bonfires of burning husks. The labour force was rarely glimpsed on these occasions, though the typical estate-owner saw himself very much as the patriarchal head of a powerful and loyal tribe of dependants.

Those families with roots going back to pre-Cession days tended to regard themselves as a special élite, the Pacific equivalent of America's founding fathers. Patricia Garvey was brought up on Taveuni, where her father was a mere doctor-cum-government officer, and she well remembers the social attitudes of the time.

In those days the planters thought they were much grander than anyone else in Fiji. At the other end of the island the people even had a racecourse. They held regular race meetings with horses which were bred by the various families. I think my father did once have a horse which he was allowed to enter in their races. Planters in those days were absolutely the lords of the land. And at the back of their houses they had these huge labour lines, the huts where the Indians lived, that to me were quite ghastly.

Even in the mid-twentieth century Jimmie MacGregor, who was head of medical services in the Solomons, found that some planters still ran their estates in their own idiosyncratic way and bitterly resented any hint of official interference.

There was one chap of Scottish extraction who played the bagpipes, I recollect, and he had a great antipathy to government in any shape or form. He would only allow certain people past his guard station. He was an ex-naval commander, I think. He had all his labour force paraded every morning for inspection in true military style, and he ran them like a regiment. It was the most spick and span plantation you could imagine. He tolerated no inefficiency, no slackness of any kind, and no visitors – not if they were government people, anyway. One of the very few people he would allow on to his property was the district doctor, which of course was how I got through.

These squirearchal eccentrics were hardly typical of the way of life of most planters. The small estate-owners lived in easy-going, down-to-earth style, on scattered homesteads tucked away between the jungle and the river, where the local gossip was handed on by bush telegraph or, in later years, through a primitive wind-up telephone system that was open to all. In Fiji, the planters' capital was the coastal settlement of Savusavu on Vanua Levu. Here at weekends most of the white residents would gather to booze and yarn the hours away at the Planters' Club, or the rickety old Hot Springs Hotel.

Prosperity generally depended on two things, the weather and the price of copra. John Goepel was a District Officer at Savusavu in the 1920s when the hard times came, and he saw a very different scene.

There was no social life then. I was there at the height of the depression, and no one had two pennies to rub together. Copra had been up to about £80 a ton during the First World War. Then it was down to about £3 15s. And so no one had any money, any whisky, anything. They were just living on boiled yams and waiting for better times.

The risks of running a plantation were infinitely greater than many novices realised. There were pitfalls in adapting to a bush way of life. Cut off from any white settlements, you could be dependent on the goodwill of the nearest native village for your survival. Yet some newcomers still expected a carefree existence, 'waiting for the coconuts to fall'.

Perhaps the worst predicament of all for an isolated planter was to be struck down with serious illness. When twenty-one-year-old Eric Muspratt first arrived on San Cristobal in 1920 to begin a six-month stint as plantation manager, he was full of enthusiasm for his South Sea adventure.

For the first time in my life I was able to dress exactly as I liked – just a pair of shorts and a belt. I just rolled into a blanket at night and rolled out of it in the morning. Here I am, I thought, young, strong, successful, living the life I love, broken away from all the mess of civilisation, the tyranny of bosses, the greed and the snobbery, the hypocrisies and stupidities, and the jangling confusion of it all. I remember quite clearly these thoughts of mine as I stood, naked and alone, in the shade of a palm tree upon one of my hilltops.

Within a few weeks he was a broken man, cut down by malaria, fighting the horrors of delirium, the violent agues and uncontrollable fevers. His weight went down from fourteen stone to ten as he lay alone on his wooden bunk, clutching a pistol to ward off nightmares. Nor did it help to be asked by his cook-boy what he wanted done with his corpse.

As it happened, Muspratt lived to write the tale, though he was a changed man in almost every way. 'Those six months in the Solomons had given me what I most wanted from life – experience. But I had paid for it in what was most precious – youth, strength, and the glamour of illusion.'

Less fortunate was the Austrian settler encountered by Tom Harrisson on a lonely island in the New Hebrides. Antonio Bruno Siller was thirty-five, a handsome aristocrat living in a tiny hut on a high cliff above the bay. His great schemes for plantations had crumbled to nothing, and he was reduced to bartering trade goods with the natives. Siller had already survived one attack of the most savage of all tropical diseases, blackwater fever. He was not to live through the next.

'I hope I will forget coming into Siller's hut the second time,' Harrisson wrote on his return visit some months later. It was sunset. 'The floor was black and teeming with the bodies of maybe forty natives, squatting there watching the big body on the bed, now vivid yellow and falling in, and the air too was alive with a few thousand bluebottle flies, who whirred an incessant orchestration . . . It took Siller seven days to die. I hope I shall never again see blackwater death.'

The real-life beachcomber had always been a far from romantic figure, and as times changed his conditions tended to become even more circumscribed, or so it seemed to Quentin Weston from his experiences as an administrator in the outlying islands of Fiji in the 1940s.

If you examine the modern beachcomber's life in detail, it wasn't very admirable, and I don't think they were respected by the Fijians. There was a man in Lau who had gone on living on one of the islands for many years after his job had been liquidated. He was living in a kind of shack. He had nothing to do. He drank a lot, there were hungry dogs all around his house, and no one seemed to take any notice of him. That was the real lot of the beachcomber, full of sores and undernourished. You weren't highly regarded by anyone – least of all yourself. A beachcomber was in fact nothing more than a parasite, who really didn't do anything effectively.

The ultimate lure for all beachcombers was the old dream of buried gold, even in Quentin Weston's day.

A man called MacCarthy went off to an island called Vatu Vara, no more than a sand-spit, where treasure was meant to have been hidden by some pirate or other. When the census came to be taken I had to visit every single island in my district and take details of everyone on them. When we got to Vatu Vara there was MacCarthy, the only inhabitant apart from a rather fearsome lady friend of his, still brooding over the idea of treasure. I think he eventually died there.

The eccentricities of these island loners never ceased to amaze their more conventional fellow countrymen. In Eric Bevington's words, 'They were not actually *troppo* but, my word, they were odd.' Some became traders, which gave them a status in the community. Almost every inhabited island had its local store, often nothing more than a wooden shack on the edge of the beach, with a tattered awning of sailcloth as shade from the midday sun. It was a vital meeting point for villagers and travellers alike, a place to pick up the local news along with a month's supply of basic provisions, and perhaps some cheap scented talcum or a length of flowered calico for the women of the family.

Although there were very few Europeans in the Gilberts, among them were some remarkable old traders who had married local women. Eric Bevington knew one who lived on lonely Kuria island.

I remember going to visit him and there was this little thatch house looking like any other Gilbertese house. But inside, it was completely lined with books, all the classics – Dickens, Shakespeare, Wordsworth, wonderful books. They were all in various stages of being eaten by insects, but nevertheless they were still obviously read. So there was this Englishman with his library, and out in front there was the trading counter, the Gilbertese woman who looked after him, and he was perfectly happy.

On Lomaloma in the Lau group lived the famous Mr Stockwell – Thomas Oswald Umphrey Stockwell – whom Quentin Weston came to know particularly well.

He came originally from Devon, and arrived at Lomaloma in 1910, where he ran the best store in the whole of the province. You could get things there which you couldn't get anywhere else. He was married to a Tongan lady of high status and she was regarded with fear and trembling by everyone in the neighbourhood.

On one occasion she was deeply offended by the Tongan medical practitioner's lack of respect for her. When next the poor man went into the Stockwell store he found himself seized by either arm by burly Tongan assistants. Then he was hit over the head with an axe handle by Mrs Stockwell.

A court case arose which I had to preside over. I found Mrs Stockwell guilty and fined her £15. Old Stockwell was absolutely appalled. From that day until he died, I was never invited to his house again.

The remittance man was another familiar figure in all British colonies, haunting the outer fringes of social and official life. By tradition, he was the black or grey sheep of the family, paid by his long-suffering relatives to keep his distance in some far-flung outpost of Empire. Alternatively, he might be a simple escapist who had chosen to ration out a small legacy on a lifetime of drifting and dreaming. Such a type was Andrew Armstrong's friend Wibberley, for example, who lived in the Polynesian Ellice Islands.

He had been an Oxford don, and he was undoubtedly a remittance man. He'd met an Ellice girl and had a large family, but he was quite a character. He used to write to the District Officers in Latin, because he was a classical scholar, and this was very annoying to some of them because they couldn't understand what he'd written.

He also had a habit of teaching the native magistrate some rather odd forms of English. The Resident Commissioner was visiting this island, and the native magistrate shook hands with him and said goodbye very politely. Then, just as the boat was about to push off, he added, 'And may the devil fly away with you, sir.' Obviously he'd been coached by Wibberley. Those were the sort of things that Wibberley thought funny, and we thought they were funny too, the first time we heard them.

Even a remittance man would occasionally take on a job, if it was not too taxing, as Quentin Weston recalls.

There was a remittance man at a tiny settlement called Londoni, on the main island of Viti Levu. He was the postmaster, and he lived in a little one-roomed house with a Fijian lady called Polly. Whenever you visited him, he used to say, 'Polly! Go down to the cellar and bring up one of the best.' And Polly would simply open a trap-door in the floor, which was on stilts, and put down a hand and bring up a bottle of home-brewed beer from underneath. He was a very well-known character.

As District Commissioner Eastern, 'Q' Weston was based at Levuka, the original white settlers' capital. When government and trade moved over to Suva on the main island, the once raffish little port became a faded shadow of itself. But it was still home for a picturesque conglomeration of Fiji's 'old identities' in the 1940s, when Weston was there.

The old-timers there were men who had come out perhaps fifty years before, with particular skills valuable in such isolated places – for instance, soap-making. There was one man who was so battered by adversity, and the sun, and everything else, that he no longer looked European at all. But in fact he was a white man who had come out and made his living from making soap. As the years went by soap began to be sold commercially, and when his particular product was no longer in demand he fell on hard times.

It was the same with another man called Neilson, who was a sail-maker. He came out in the days when all the cutters were powered entirely by canvas and didn't have auxilary engines at all. He was a wonderful craftsman and still at work repairing and so on, even though the demand for sails had declined so greatly.

Just occasionally these people would feel the urge to return to the land of their birth, if only for a brief nostalgic visit. A man called Mayne, for instance, who had been in the islands since before the First World War, finally got retirement leave after thirty years' service with the trading firm of Morris Hedstrom. The whole community turned out to give him a tremendous send-off as he embarked on the first stage of the long sea journey home to his native Cornwall. 'See you in a year!' he told his friends. Four weeks later they were welcoming him back again. Mr Mayne had only got as far as New Zealand before he decided that the shock of the new was too much for him, and back he hastened to the peaceful cocoon of Levuka.

As for a certain Dr Beattie, no one quite knew what kind of a doctor he was. According to Quentin Weston, he looked 'extremely like a parrot', was a very keen churchman and had married, late in life, a missionary lady whom he had introduced rather too successfully to the delights of gin.

But the real drama of Beattie's life came, so to speak, soon after his death.

Mrs Beattie rang me up and said she had been having terrible dreams. Her husband had been telling her that he had been buried the wrong way round. That is, instead of facing with his feet to the east – as should have been the case – he was facing west. As a strict fundamentalist, he was absolutely horrified that at the second coming he would be facing the wrong direction. She went on ringing up regularly, saying not only that these dreams were continuing, but that she would not cease consuming gin until her husband was safely and comfortably buried the right way round, and would I please see to it.

This involved a very complicated procedure, because you couldn't just dig graves up and turn people round. In due course an order, signed by the Governor, arrived and we dug him up. Incredibly enough, he *was* buried the wrong way round, so we turned him, filled up the grave again, and I wrote off my report to the Governor. I also reported to Mrs Beattie that her husband's orders had been carried out. But the extraordinary thing was that, from that day onwards, Mrs Beattie never touched another drop of gin.

12
Invasion

From the mid-1930s onwards, the threat of war hovered over the placid existence of the British in the South Seas. The battles for the islands that lay in the path of Japanese imperial conquest were enacted among the vast seascapes and the fragile communications networks of a world very different from Europe. The strategies and the dramas of these battles are recorded in detail in the official records of the war in the Pacific, but the scattered fragments of personal experience help to convey the reality of that extraordinary time:

Ronald Garvey was sent by government to Ocean Island to put the Gilbert and Ellice colony 'on a wartime footing', and in December 1941 he found himself in the firing line right at the opening of hostilities.

It was the day that the Japanese attacked the fleet in Pearl Harbour. By 8 a.m. two or three planes were coming down from the Japanese mandated islands to the north. Having spotted Ocean Island, and I suppose the Union Jack flying in front of the Residency, they decided they'd better bomb it. They pattern-bombed my residence with about eighteen bombs. I escaped with a superficial wound. I think I was the only person who ever shed a drop of blood in the days when I was still in charge of Ocean Island, before we had to evacuate it.

Anyhow, when the Japanese planes had left we walked round the Residency, which was a sorry sight. The upstairs was blown downstairs, and the downstairs was blown upstairs, but there was one thing which tremendously impressed all the natives. In the dining-room hung a large portrait of King George VI, and whatever else the Japanese bombs may have achieved, that picture was on the wall utterly and absolutely intact. Right from the start this gave the local people the firm impression that nothing would defeat the King.

It soon became clear to Ronald Garvey that Ocean was only the first stop on the Japanese bombing circuit.

They used to come over every day. They would drop five bombs on Ocean Island, and then they'd go round back by the Solomon Islands and they would drop the last three on the headquarters at Tulagi. This went on for a long time, and I thought it was damned unfair. I knew that the Japanese had got the GTC – the General Telegraph Code – because it was not very secret. So I thought that, if I put out a message in the GTC, they might pick this one up. So I telegraphed my High Commissioner in Suva, Sir Harry Luke, and explained to him that these planes were coming round, dropping five bombs on us and only three on the Solomon Islands. I added that I'd always thought that there was something sporting about the Japanese, but apparently I'd been completely mistaken. Within a week, the Solomon Islands got five bombs and we got three!

With the Japanese invasion of the northern Gilberts soon after-wards, Ocean Island was evacuated and the Solomons became the next focus of attack. Over the months that followed, that sprawling range of densely forested Melanesian heartland was to prove the major battleground of the war in the Pacific.

In 1942, with Singapore about to fall, it was evident to the British that a full-scale defence of the territory was out of the question. As many expatriates as possible were sent by sea to Australia, under dangerous and crowded conditions. At the same time, the Japanese were advancing down from the northern part of the Solomons, and the administration moved to a secret headquarters in a remote corner of one of the outer islands. Officially, the motto was 'business as usual' and the islanders were reassured that, as far as possible, the government they had known for over fifty years would still be in control.

For the British administrators it was a confusing and frustrating time. Some became part of an impromptu and ill-equipped Defence Force. Others left to enrol in Australia. Then, as the Allies prepared for a counter-invasion, American submarines began a cautious investigation of the occupied coasts. It seemed obvious to David Trench that no one knew the terrain better than the District Officer. 'With some difficulty' he persuaded the High Commissioner to let him join a beach reconnaisance expedition which was to survey the Shortlands group for possible landing sites. As happened so often with this kind of warfare, nothing went quite according to plan.

The idea was that when the submarine got opposite this gap in the reef where we were supposed to land, I was to look through the periscope and tell them where we were. Well now, we hadn't practised this. And when we came to the point, I found, first of all, that I couldn't focus the periscope down to my short sight, and secondly, I couldn't get my glasses inside the hood of the eyepieces. So we had to assume where we were by dead reckoning, and when night came, mine was the first party to be dropped and off we paddled in our little rubber boats.

We were supposed to be paddling on a magnetic bearing, on a compass. Now if you fill a small rubber boat with a lot of heavily armed marines and try and steer on a compass bearing, you're going to be pretty wildly wrong, because the amount of hardware in the boat is going to throw the compass entirely off. So we found we were about five miles from where we should have been – opposite another break in the reef, where two other boats were supposed to have landed. In the end, we all landed in the same spot.

Next, our instructions were to hide the boat. Well, you try and dig a hole the size of a rubber boat in a few minutes flat! But we hid it as best we could.

Then I took my party up the beach towards the landing site, walking along in the moonlight with our feet in the surf, so that there wouldn't be any footprints. I had with me a Solomon Islander I knew very well, Sergeant Ilala, who was a marvellous tracker, and a marvellous bushman. He went forward under cover and found that the site was already occupied by three large guns and a very considerable number of Japanese. But he got right in amongst those guns, counted them and even came back with the measurements. In fact if we had landed at the right place, we would have paddled our little rubber boats right up the muzzles of the Japanese artillery. So that was a bit lucky.

Even more extraordinary were the experiences of a small group of administrators who infiltrated behind enemy lines and lived in hiding for up to two years. These were the legendary coast-watchers. As young District Officers, their initiation into the rigours of administering some of the wildest country in the world had prepared them well for their new roles as guerilla leaders and spotters. Hidden high up in the jungle with their Solomon Island patrols, it was their task to transmit to headquarters vital information on Japanese movements.

Nick Waddell was an original member of this 'invisible army' and remembers that the first hazard was the actual embarkation. 'Instead of landing on a white sandy beach, as we'd expected, we had to make it over a coral reef. We had three months' stores to carry with us and we spent the rest of the night crawling over those jagged potholes, after which we sagged with sheer exhaustion into the bush and went to sleep with no lookout, nothing.'

The island was Choiseul, in the northern Solomons, and as luck would have it their footprints were spotted next morning by a Choiseulman called Beni, who was an old friend of Waddell's. Eager to help, he set off down the coast to find a couple of island policemen who were also known to Waddell.

Back they came within twenty-four hours and helped us get our stores off the beach, up into the first hill behind. Then we got a radio station going, and began to report on the Japanese movements, which were fairly considerable. Ten miles away they had a radio station of their own, as well as a couple of platoons of soldiers, doing the same thing we were doing, reporting any enemy movements. When we got on the air, of course, it didn't take long for them to realise that there was something going on. Then there was a report that they were very near, so we had to get out of the back door quickly.

Deep in that jungle, there were other hidden perils – the trailing loia vine whose tentacles could rip great holes in the flesh, the giant centipede whose bite meant three days of feverish agony. But this kind of bush-trekking was second nature to the Solomon Islanders, who used to enjoy conducting forays of their own against the enemy.

They used to play games with the Japs, whenever they spotted one of their little broadcasting shacks. When the man inside came off duty, my scouts realised that the shack was empty for about ten minutes while he went down the path to meet the next chap coming on duty. So my scouts managed to get in there, and first of all began removing spare parts. Then after that, they got bold and they moved whole transmitters. The Japs were furious but they could never catch them.

On Rendova, in the centre of the group, Dick Horton, now a coast-watcher too, also found himself almost totally dependent on the support of the local people.

I was stationed there to watch the airstrip at Munda and to do what damage I could. I was only a mile from the Japs for nine months, and my marvellous Solomon Islanders never let me down. They never gave away anything. That, I think, was about as tricky a time as I ever had. I was living in the bush, way up in the jungle. I had a marvellous old man who was too fragile to do anything else but catch fish, and he caught fish for me. Otherwise I lived on fern tops and coconuts, and K ration whenever I could get it.

From time to time there was a direct confrontation with the enemy, as Nick Waddell recalls.

We spotted about sixteen Japs sitting on a river bank just behind our camp. They'd come up through the bush and were only about a mile or two away. They had stacked all their weapons to one side. Very quietly my marksmen circled them round and then just let fly. Fortunately they hit a grenade or two that the Japs were wearing on their belts, so it was a totally clean sweep. But it was a justified one from our point of view, in the sense that they were threatening our observation post and would have destroyed it and us.

The District Officers were not the only Britishers who had gone into hiding. Although many of the missionaries had been evacuated from the Solomons, some had elected to stay on, despite the stories of Japanese atrocities inflicted on mission workers elsewhere in the Pacific. In February 1942 a government order came: 'All white women out!' But for nuns and teachers scattered up and down the islands there was the all-important task of getting the children to places of safety, as the machine gun fire rattled among the cliffs, and from the Bishop's verandah came the beating of the alarm drum which meant: 'Go bush at once.'

'Going bush' was the escape route for Christine Woods and her two fellow nurses when a Japanese landing force was sighted approaching the mission hospital on Malaita.

We were just wondering what we were going to do, when round the corner came fifteen sorry-looking men who'd escaped from the neighbouring island of Gela. Could they come with us? We said, 'Yes, indeed you can!' We were absolutely delighted to see them, because we had to walk two days up into the bush to get right into the top, out of the way of the Japs. We had to cross three rivers which were in flood, and when we got to the first river the water was rushing down and it looked impassable. So what did they do? A couple of them swam to the other side, they cut down some vines, swam back and tied them on to a tree our side. And the fifteen men hung onto that rope in the river while we crawled across their shoulders. We had to do that three times that day.

Eventually we got to this village right at the very top of Malaita, and the people gave us a couple of huts, fed us and so on. But when we'd rested up a bit we said, 'Look now, we must make some other arrangement. We don't want to be in the village, because if the Japs do get up here and they find you've helped us, you'll be in trouble. Can you give us a place where we're right away from you?' So they took us down to a bamboo grove. The leaves of bamboo only grow at the top, so it was a marvellous cover. You couldn't see anything at all from the sky. Right in the middle they built us a little house, all in a day – really primitive, but it was ours.

The first night, I must have slept for about an hour when I opened my eyes, and I was absolutely petrified. There was no front to the house, no doors at all, and as I looked out I saw we were surrounded by lights. I whispered to the others that we had to get out. We always kept a bundle ready for immediate escape, and so we grabbed our bundles and got out through the back. The walls were made of bamboo and tied with a bit of string, so we only had to cut that and pull out a few canes to get through. Luckily we had bush all round us and we just dived into it.

Then we looked back, and those lights were still exactly in the same position, not moving at all. We stood there for about twenty minutes or so watching them, until we got brave and went slowly back towards them. They were all at different heights, and do you know what it was? Fungi. Pieces of fungi on the trees. They were as brilliant as anything, because it was a pitch-black night with no moon or anything and the stars were beautiful, and there was this great glow all around us, completely phosphorescent!

Japanese methods of retaliation were swift and brutal towards any islanders found to be helping the British. Even the withholding of information on the whereabouts of white men brought risk of appalling penalties. Anti-white racial propaganda was also applied relentlessly by the enemy, while food gardens were looted and villages wrecked without discrimination. But the loyalty of the people remained unshaken and many examples of great personal courage were recorded. As Christine Woods recalls, one of the Melanesian missionaries proved himself particularly skilful at games of bluff with the Japanese officers.

Next door to the Japs, down on the mission station, was one of our priests, a man called George Kieria. The Jap Colonel went down to Father George one day and said, 'Father, we must learn this language of yours. We want to make friends with the people.'

So George went down to the camp for about a week, teaching simple sentences. About four or five days later, the Colonel came to George's house and said, 'Father George, the Melanesian people really hard to make friends. Every time we go for talk to people, everybody run away.'

It was only later that Father George told me what he was really teaching the Japs. He said, 'I teach 'em one sentence, Sister. "You fella come anywhere near, we shoot you!"'

The islanders' general attitude to the Japanese was one of scorn. A certain song in pidgin English, describing each Japanese defeat at the hands of the Americans, became a wartime hit. Every verse ended with the derisive line, 'Me laugh along you, Japani! Ha, ha!'

With the progress of the Allied counter-offensive through 1942 and 1943, the American forces developed their famous leapfrog tactics, moving up northwards through the Solomons, driving the Japanese before them along the path of their original invasion. At the forefront of the offensive was the battle of Guadalcanal. Ten thousand American marines were landed on the island, and over-night the sandy bays and blue lagoons were blotted out by some of the most dramatic battle scenes of the war. David Trench still finds it surprising how little the people in Britain know about the ferocity and the scale of the fighting in that part of the world, particularly the naval battles.

I happened to be on the ridges behind Guadalcanal, just off the beach at a little elevation, when the battle of 13 November took place. It was night action. The American heavy cruisers went in against Japanese battleships, and you could actually see the firing on both sides – see the fall of shot on both sides – because the battle was fought at ridiculously close range. I don't think you could have seen capital ships in action against each other like that at any time since perhaps the battle of the Nile.

For any airman shot down by the Japanese over the islands, the most likely fate was to be hunted down by the enemy. Crash landing at sea, miles from anywhere, he could expect to meet death by drowning or starvation. There was only one slight hope, and that was to be picked up by a canoe from a neighbouring island. But the local people, however anxious to help, needed the support of a full-scale rescue service to get the wounded to the nearest medical post and the uninjured back to one of the Allied bases. It was another task for the Government Defence Force. With the help of officers such as Nick Waddell, some quite remarkable feats of survival were achieved.

Our base was a collecting centre for ditched American fliers. We had to take them down the coast to the rendezvous fifty or sixty miles away where there was sufficient harbour space for the flying boats to land. This was on the Japanese barge route connecting from New Georgia up to Choiseul Bay and then across to Shortlands.

The Japanese mostly travelled by night and holed up during the day, so we did the opposite. We travelled by day, by a middle-sized canoe, not too big to attract attention, about the size that an ordinary fisherman or villager would use. We'd have a crew of maybe four or five islanders, and if there were more than two Americans we had to have two canoes. While we were usually safe enough from any attack from the land, we weren't secure from the air. So when the prospecting aircraft flew over, we had to hastily conceal ourselves under the palm fronds and fish. Passing the Japanese shore encampments you had to do the same, because we would have been hunted down the minute anyone had seen a white face in a canoe otherwise filled with coconuts.

Waddell's partner in these exploits was former plantation manager called Seton. He was a bearded giant of a man and fairly skilled in medical matters. From their hideaway, Seton looked after both the local population and the injured Americans – among them a Marine Corps pilot by the name of Bill Coffine, whose story was typical.

He was shot down in the 'Slot', between Choiseul and Ysabel. He eventually got ashore in a lot of uninhabited islands and paddled around there for days looking for help. He survived for thirty-five days, not having seen a soul. Towards the end he managed to catch a bird and also got one or two flying fish that landed into his rubber dinghy, but that's all.

He was picked up by scouts who had a regular patrol, and when they brought him the seventy miles up the coast to where we were this poor chap was nothing but skin and bone, and suffering terribly from exposure, of course. Seton took care of him and we fed him up, but it took six weeks before he was really mobile.

A thousand miles to the north-east, up in the Gilbert and Ellice colony, the main island of Tarawa had been in Japanese hands since December 1941 and was to remain so until 20 November 1943. During those two years of occupation, the Europeans who had elected to stay behind – government officials, traders and missionaries – were treated with the utmost brutality. Twenty-two of them, after being held in internment, were rounded up and murdered in cold blood.

The Ellice Islands escaped occupation altogether, and even in the Gilberts the invading forces only got as far as the northern part of the group. Nevertheless any drifting survivors of enemy action in this part of the Pacific could count themselves lucky to land on one of the outer islands where the British were still in control. James Coode was District Officer on Beru when one such survivor was, almost literally, washed up on his doorstep.

I was sitting in my little bungalow one evening and a very excited Gilbert Islander ran in and said, 'There's a strange European who's come from the ocean side.' That was the side of the island that was open to the weather and regarded as an impossible landing. Shortly after that, in came a rather battered-looking American, and I was absolutely astonished to see him. He and his friends had been shipwrecked and had been thirty days at sea in a lifeboat.

Having been torpedoed off Hawaii, they'd made it right across to the Gilberts and crash landed on Nukunau, the next island to mine. The Americans had been so thrilled to see land that they'd gone as far as they could on to it, hit the reef and turned right over. They all had to get out pretty quickly from underneath, staggered ashore and then the people of Nukunau looked after them.

I always remember when I was over there with them, one of them said to me, quite innocently, 'You come from the big village, I expect. Now you see these sores? Could you buy some Germolene ointment? You can get it at any drug store, just fifty cents.'

Right from the start of the war, it was feared that the chief prize of the Japanese offensive would be the crown colony of Fiji which was the central hub of the British territorial network in the Pacific. Even before the outbreak of hostilities, Japanese ships coming through the group were suspected of spying activities to detect the readiness or otherwise of the defence system. For this reason an elaborate hoax was staged by the British, a famous bluff that is still remembered by Alastair Forbes, who was resident magistrate in the capital, Suva.

It seems that the colony's defences were operating on a shoe-string and, although there was a battery above the town, it was well known that the range of its guns failed to extend to the most vital point of all, the entrance in through the reef. Only a six-inch gun would cover the distance. One night, when the Japanese were in harbour, a mysterious ship arrived from New Zealand and was escorted in at midnight by a convoy. There were blackout restrictions in operation. But somehow or other, just as the ship was rounding in, close up to the Japanese vessel, someone on board struck a match or two for a cigarette.

The light shone on a large gun barrel. By next morning everybody knew that a six-inch gun had arrived and been installed at the battery which could cover the entrance through the reef. But not a whisper got out until after the war that this was a wooden gun. Lighting the cigarette and everything else was absolutely deliberate.

For colonial officials such as Forbes, it was soon evident that Suva itself was particularly vulnerable to Japanese invasion plans.

A kind of Home Guard was formed and I had a mixed platoon of Chinese, Fijians and Europeans. It was a bit like Dad's Army, but we used to go out and do exercises, and we had the occasional alarm. I'm glad to say they were not for real, any of them, and it'd have been very uncomfortable if they had been, because the place was really completely indefensible.

With the occupation of the Solomons, the threat of invasion grew more real. As District Officer for the western side of the main island of Viti Levu, Philip Snow had to put into operation a variety of unlikely-sounding government plans to deal with possible overnight landing by the Japanese.

One of them was to have the Fijians of neighbouring villages protect, or at least safeguard as well as they could, the bridges on the roads close to the airport. The Fijians took all this organising as a great joke. I would give them yellow armbands which said BG, meaning Bridge Guard. That of course meant nothing to them in their language. They had no weapons at all, except fishing spears. However, they entered into the spirit of the thing in their usual way.

One day the message came from New Zealand Army Headquarters that the Japanese were on their way to Fiji. So I had to dash round in my car, no lights on but a brilliant moon as usual – rousing the villages and mobilising these Bridge Guards. I took along lots of cigarettes, because they'd be up all night, and they began enjoying themselves, blacking their faces with the sort of warpaint that they used for their dances. Then they took up their positions near the bridges, armed with their spears.

Fortunately the Japanese never came, otherwise the Fijians would never have had a chance. They'd have been mown down by machine gun fire without ever having had a glimpse of the enemy. But they had the utmost contempt for them. The Fijians couldn't believe that they weren't a match for any number of Japanese, had they come.

As it happened, the Fijians were able to prove their point when three commando battalions, led by their chiefs and a number of European officers, were dispatched to the Solomons and made an international name for themselves as jungle fighters.

In Fiji itself, the long-feared Japanese invasion never materialised. Instead, as Len Usher remembers, there soon appeared a much more welcome army of occupation.

During the war we had something like 50,000 troops constantly in Fiji – first New Zealanders and then, after Pearl Harbour, they were replaced by Americans. Now if you drop 50,000 'drunken and licentious soldiery' into a society such as Fiji's, you create quite a number of social problems. They commandeered houses. We had a curfew. There were food shortages, there was rationing and all that sort of thing. I must say, I think we dealt with them very well, but then it seems to me typical of Fiji to be able to handle race relations well.

Dora Patterson, descendant of a long-established settler family, was living in Levuka at the time and she saw the little ghost town come to life again with this influx of young fighting men.

Well, I shouldn't say it, but it was one of the happiest times for Levuka. They used the town as a holiday place for the army. My husband and his brother ran the picture shows in the town hall and the government asked them to put on something extra to entertain the soldiers. So after the films the chairs were all put away, the dancing would begin and we would go on till about one o'clock in the morning, and the next night would be the same. I lost a lot of weight dancing. My husband took me along every night and we had a wonderful time. American airmen came here too and quite a few of them were billeted by my sister and my father at any house that had room, because the hotel just couldn't handle them all. The New Zealand army rented a whole house here for their personnel, and the girls had a wonderful time, I tell you. Not only girls, but married ladies, too. But it was terrible to say you had a good time out of a war. Those boys, the ones we danced with, would go away and perhaps never be heard of again.

Throughout the islands the mood of the times had broken down the old codes of custom, to a certain extent at least. Some spots in the Pacific had a special appeal for lonely American airmen. Around the lagoon of Sikaiana in the Solomons, for instance, an island famous for its beautiful women, so many seaplanes were reporting out of action, due to engine failure, that the admiral ordered a special survey to see if some kind of topographical feature was responsible. It is said that when the low-flying aerial photographs were processed, they turned out to be some of the most revealing reconnaissance shots of the war.

Inevitably, in the towns and villages, a legacy was left that Queen Salote in Tonga always referred to as our 'little souvenirs of the war'. The sudden outcrop of fair-skinned and sometimes blond-haired Polynesian and Melanesian babies was a visible reminder of the *entente* between the military and civilian populations, and an incident related by Alastair Forbes no doubt had its counterparts throughout the South Pacific. 'Towards the end of the war the local District Commissioner was on his rounds and came across a Fijian girl with a noticeably light-coloured baby. He admired the baby and asked, "Who's the father – American or New Zealand?" and she said, "I don't know, he hasn't spoken yet."

On the surface, the local people everywhere had adapted with surprising ease to all the upheavals of the war. But at another level, some far-reaching changes were taking place which were to affect the whole future of the British in the Pacific. There was the thrill of final victory and jubilation everywhere on 15 August 1945, the day when 'the Nips threw in the sponge'. But some subtle balance between the rulers and the ruled had been disturbed for ever. The islanders had seen their all-powerful government threatened and humiliated by a ruthless invading force. They had seen the law-makers and the peace-keepers from Britannia suddenly vulnerable, dependant for their lives on the local people and on the huge armies of another white nation.

There was a final contradiction that went deeper still. Allen and Elizabeth Rutter were working on their remote mission station in the Solomons when war came. Their radio set was often out of order, eaten up by ants and cockroaches, but they passed on news to the villages of the German onslaught on Europe through the newspapers that arrived two months late from Sydney. Then the horrors of modern warfare erupted on to their own beaches.

The native people were totally perplexed. They said, 'We don't understand the white man. You came to us and said, "Put away your bows and arrows and your spears. You can live at peace." So we did live at peace. What's the matter with the white man who knows this is the truth? Here he is shooting bombs down from the air and blowing up ships from under the sea. We fought man to man. You're killing women and children who don't even see where the enemy is.' They found the whole thing a very puzzling experience, and, of course, there was no answer.

13
Waiting for the Cargo

It was in the Melanesian territories of the Solomons and the New Hebrides that wartime experiences produced the strangest effects. In less than a single generation, the people had been expected to make the leap from a Stone Age culture to a materialist civilisation of huge complexity. The invading waves of the 1940s, both hostile and friendly, had only accelerated the process of disorientation. The most dramatic symptom of this general unrest was the growth of what were known as cargo cults.

In the Solomons there was a very militant movement by the name of Marching Rule. It started on Malaita, a place always noted for what government called 'unruly elements', but quickly spead to other islands. As a teaching priest with the Melanesian mission, Derek Rawcliffe came into contact with Marching Rule in 1947 and learned first-hand from the local people what its message was.

The idea was that the American troops had not all gone away. They were hidden up in the bush, waiting for the day when they would come down and kill all the British. Then shiploads of cargo would arrive for the people. The way they saw it was quite simple. Europeans have all kinds of wonderful things, and of course they don't make any of them, because Europeans don't do any work. So they must come from the underworld, where the ancestors are. It's the ancestors who supply all these things, which should come to us. But the Europeans have taken them all. So what do we do to get more cargo? Well, we see for example that the European talks into a box with a wire going from it. He says, 'The ship is calling tomorrow.' And sure enough the ship comes tomorrow. And so we make a box and we put up a stick with a wire on it, and we talk into the box, and we hope that the cargo will come.

In the New Hebrides the cult had a definite figurehead, the mysterious prophet John Frum. All enquiries as to his identity were dismissed or evaded, though some said the name derived from the nickname of one of the wartime soldiers, 'John-from-America'. But as Guy Wallington remembers from his days as an administrator, there was no mistaking the symbols of the faith, which could crop up alongside any lonely path or small bush village.

You'd see them before you got there, these red-painted wooden crosses and red gates. In one or two places there might be a carving, a rough one, of an aeroplane or even of a figure, always with a whitish face. This was the Messiah who was going to come.

In the meantime, they'd be waiting for the submarines or whatever was going to bring all kinds of riches. When they found they didn't come, eventually disillusionment set in amongst some of the John Frum followers. They didn't all go back to the missions, but they went to the old customs instead, or started what one might call a neo-paganism, which was a mixture of beliefs.

Over the years, the cult dwindled away. In the Solomons, though, Marching Rule developed into a powerful political movement, anti-European in sentiment and preaching a message of non-cooperation with the government and the missionaries. The people stopped paying their taxes. They built stockades around their villages, complete with watch-towers on the lines of the American camps. Many of them destroyed their food gardens after they were told they would not be needed 'when the cargo comes'. Marching Rule communities sprang up in one island after another, and more than once British administrators such as Tom Russell found themselves threatened by an armed uprising.

The occasion I remember in 1949 was at Auki, the District Headquarters, where there was to be a very large meeting. Several thousand people were gathered together and they wanted to tell the District Commissioner about their grievances. Above all they wanted to announce that they were independent, and that wages had to be increased – six- or sevenfold, automatically, overnight.

There was the District Commissioner, one other District Officer and myself to face the music. This crowd simply closed round about us, armed with all sorts of native weapons, as well as shotguns and some wartime rifles kept in reserve in one of the nearby villages. They had a very clever orator, a man called

Eriel Billy. He started off on the grievances and periodically turned to the crowd to say, 'Have I told you the truth?' And they'd all say 'Ee-o!' which was 'Yes.' And then he came on to the demands – independence immediately and so on – and each time he'd say, 'Is that what we want?' And the crowd went 'Ee-o!' He really worked them up, and a crowd of that kind is a flash point.

Then Monty Marston, who was District Commissioner, got to his feet and said very slowly and ponderously, 'You know, you've raised a lot of things of substantial importance today. You obviously don't expect me to give an instant decision. I'll have to write a letter to Headquarters.' There was silence. 'This is it,' I thought. Then Marston said, 'Well, time for tea.' The three of us walked into the crowd and it parted before us. We went up to the District Commissioner's house and sat on the verandah and had tea and cucumber sandwiches, and the crowd danced around for a bit and eventually disappeared.

At first, the response of the colonial authorities was fairly traditional. Non-payment of taxes, for instance, was punished with prison sentences. However, it soon became clear that a new policy was needed, as Derek Rawcliffe recounts.

They realised they were getting nowhere, and there was a better way of doing things. They set up a local council and made the organisers of this movement the leaders. Many of us said at the time that was just giving way to them and government was wrong. But in fact it was the wisest thing they could have done, because that was really what the people were looking for – some kind of control over their own affairs. So as these local councils took off, the Marching Rule movement just fizzled out.

Nevertheless, all over the Pacific the basic message remained the same. The wonders of Western technology – the radio sets, the tinned food, the trucks, the boat engines and so on – had been made suddenly available to them in time of war. To turn the clock back and do without them again was asking the impossible.

By the same process, their own few prize possessions had become strangely devalued and trivialised. In Fiji, for example, the GIs became expert at acquiring the hereditary war clubs that were often masterpieces of the wood-carver's art, as well as the historic badges of chiefly conquest. Robert Lever remembers how, when stocks threatened to run out, 'the Americans had very bright engineers, and every time they heard that a new unit was due from the States they got busy turning out facsimile clubs that were sold to the soldiers as the real thing. Genuine GI warclubs, they should have been called.'

The sacred whales' teeth known as *tambua*, the focal point of every Fijian ceremony, were even more popular wartime souvenirs. Eventually government issued an edict banning their export from the country, but not before a serious shortage made itself felt in every corner of the islands. Jane Roth tells the story of how a resourceful Secretary for Fijian Affairs filled the gap.

> He was home on leave and found there were whales' teeth available in Aberdeen, of all places. He brought several cases of them back with him and the Fijian women got to work on them, oiling and polishing them into shape and transforming them into *tambua*, complete with cords. In no time at all they were put into circulation and Fijian custom was safely preserved, thanks to Scotland!

The gradual changeover from the old barter systems to a monetary economy in Fiji affected the way of life of both the islanders and those in authority such as Quentin Weston. A wage packet could buy an iron roof for a house instead of thatch, tinned salmon from Canada instead of fresh fish, and imported rice and bread.

> In this way, the people themselves became much more materialistic. They cut their famous fuzzy hair and became very much the European. One can't blame them, because everyone said that is what they should do. Their attitude to government changed, too. The particular privileged position which the District Officer used to have was gradually eroded by a much more critical approach. If he didn't produce the goods in the form of a road here and there, or some kind of development scheme for the area, then he wasn't doing his job properly.

Everywhere the white administrator was no longer a symbol of divine authority who could do no wrong. In the Solomons, the islanders had fought alongside these seemingly all-powerful figures and from the shared experiences of danger and hardship had come a new kind of personal closeness. In northern Malaita, Tom Russell was frequently on tour in the bush, where his status as a District Officer was no bar to friendship.

> You'd be out on patrol for a fortnight at a time and you'd have

maybe fifteen or twenty Solomon Islanders in your party. At night, you were put up in whatever housing there was in a village, and you all mucked in together. You ate the same things, you cut some banana leaves, put them down on the floor, and that was your bed. You had a blanket in your pack, but it was all very primitive, and you were simply treated as one of them. They'd be joking with each other about their girl-friends and their sexual prowess and so on, and you could chip in and rib them the same as they were ribbing each other, and you felt very close.

There were changing attitudes among the wives of the administrators too. A young woman coming out from post-war Britain would feel much less obliged to take on the role of a minor memsahib than her predecessors who, even in the carefree South Seas, paid due deference to the rites of coffee mornings, afternoon bridge and servant problems if they lived in the towns and capitals of the territories. For those who were fortunate or interested enough to go on tour with their husbands into the more remote corners of the islands, there was often a chance to shed the role completely, as Rita McGregor found when they were visiting the Polynesian outpost of Sikaiana.

The first day I went ashore I was dressed in a frock and played the lady, walking up and down admiring the view. But the next day I just went ashore in my *sulu* – a sort of cotton wrap like a sarong that the women wore. On the beach they were loading the copra on to canoes, to be taken out to where the ship had anchored some distance away. I had got to know one of the local girls, and so I began helping her carry the copra. It was on strings and you loaded it over your shoulder, carried it down to the water's edge and dumped it in the canoes. When her canoe was full she motioned to me to get inside and she sat at the back and off we paddled across the reef. At least, I thought we were both paddling until I looked round. There was she sitting in the back with her arms folded, laughing at me.

Some administrative officers went straight from war service to postings in the Pacific. Kelvin Nicholson left the navy in 1946 to join the Colonial Service, and his appointment as DO of the Line Islands took him to three of the loneliest specks in the Pacific – Fanning, Washington and Christmas, just above the Equator – where he was variously plantation manager, wireless operator, tax-collector, postmaster and magistrate, among other jobs. Officially the islands were part of the Gilberts, and Nicholson was able to establish the kind of rapport with the Gilbertese that was typical of the post-war era.

> This is why I think we were so lucky, those of us who came into the Service at that particular time. You were dealing with people who said simply, 'You're Europeans, you know all about things like radios and trucks. We know all about fishing and coconuts and living on these islands, so we can learn from each other.' In other words, you got on at a level of equality which was marvellous.

Later on, at Tarawa, one of the innovations for which Nicholson was responsible was the start of a local broadcasting system, with regular vernacular programmes. Closely connected with this was his work on the introduction of the Co-operative Movement, which was to take over the marketing of copra and other products, and even set up its own retail stores.

In the medical field, too, a sense of achievement was becoming possible in these changing times. A government doctor such as Jimmie McGregor, who'd worked in the remote villages of the Solomons, could trace a clear pattern of progress from the conditions of the 1920s and 1930s.

> Death was a regular visitor then, as it was in nineteenth-century Britain, so much so that the people in some parts didn't name their babies for the first year. Tuberculosis was rife, particularly in the Polynesian groups. Leprosy was pretty prevalent and yaws was of course a major problem – that was cleared up during the period we were there through penicillin injections. With the help of the World Health Organisation, we took steps to clean up malaria, and we were very successful – so much so that, whereas children had been dying at a very great rate, as time went by the villages became overpopulated, began to teem with healthy kids and the Director of Education was complaining bitterly because he had insufficient resources to cope with this population explosion. Years later, on one of his visits, the Duke of Edinburgh took the islanders to task for having one of the highest growth rates in the world. Really, he should have been addressing his remarks to me and my medical colleagues.

Anne Sopper, travelling round the islands as a field officer for the British Red Cross, found that the names of this new generation of children had kept pace with the times. 'Tin Can,

Label and X-Ray were three I remember especially. There was also a small boy who had been christened Pope-John – by a Presbyterian family as it happened. There were some new pidgin words too – perhaps the best was their expression for the Bishop's helicopter: Big Fella Mixmaster Belong God.'

The sight of an intrepid woman on the horizon, bearing strange gifts and even stranger items of information, was nothing new to the islanders. A hundred years before, the wives of ship's captains or missionaries had been eager to demonstrate the niceties of quilt embroidery, or the cultivation of a flower garden, with a lecture on the evils of polygamy thrown in on the side. Now, in the 1950s and 1960s, it was called Community Relations. Specially appointed advisors and inspectors toured the islands and made their progress reports to the Colonial Office. One of the most influential was Freda Gwilliam, a specialist in women's education and in the setting-up of the kind of women's organisations that were hitherto unheard of in the isolated villages of Melanesia and Polynesia.

Young recruits to Voluntary Service Overseas began to arrive, sent to turn their hand to any kind of job. Among them, as Freda Gwilliam remembers, was an English girl only just out of school, who found herself confronted by some daunting responsibilities.

When she disembarked, she was met by two rather weary Methodist missionaries and invited to 'meet the staff'. It turned out she was to be the head of a school of thirty-six children and three Solomon Island teachers with only four years' schooling themselves. Her gaiety and liveliness, however, soon worked miracles, and then after about three months she was informed that she was also Inspector of Schools, and the time had come to go on a tour of the islands. Just when she had assimilated this idea, they added, 'By the way, can you deliver a baby?' It seems that the Inspector was also expected to deal with any medical emergencies that were encountered in the villages. Anyway, she was given a quick briefing on midwifery and a medical box and off she set. On her return, the proudest item on her report was: 'Delivery of one eight-pound baby boy, mother and child both doing well.'

Because of the cataclysm of the war new ideas took root more easily, and in the major centres the educational curricula grew increasingly sophisticated. In Fiji's Queen Victoria School, an enterprising young master such as Graham Leggatt was able to kindle a particular enthusiasm for performances of Shakepeare.

They took to Shakespeare like ducks to water. They loved the rhetoric – the Fijians are great orators – and of course in a play like *Macbeth* there was so much that was parallel to their own history – the tribal wars and the assassinations of rival chieftains and so on. We did have one or two problems with these muscular young men playing the female roles. There was a Lady Macbeth who was marching along with six-foot strides, and I got round that one by tying his ankles together with a length of string, so that he was confined to a rather more lady-like pace.

After the school performance, the production went on tour round the villages.

A lot of the people really didn't know much English, but they would come up in great strength and sit and watch enthralled. After the show, the village would turn on a big performance for us – there would be a feast and a *yanggona* ceremony, and then dancing all night. I remember the dancing going on in one of these Fijian houses and by the end of the evening there was no floor left. It had just been trampled underfoot. It was great fun, and they were great times.

14
Farewell to Eden

Times were changing, but it was often hard to believe it. The British knew that the end was somewhere in sight – just over the horizon, a few years away, maybe ten, maybe more. But there was a sense of timelessness about the South Seas that always seemed to push the future away. *Malua* was the Fijian word for it – 'by and by' . . . Even in those post-war years there were still islands where there was no such thing as a clock and the only record of the passing hours was the sun overhead.

The sense of personal isolation, too, was still part of everyday life if, like Kelvin Nicholson, you were posted to 'a remote little speck way out south of Honolulu'. Communications on Fanning Island had changed little since the nineteenth century, and as sole representative of the British Crown he took on his responsibilities with true Victorian seriousness.

We only got one ship every couple of years from the Gilberts, a recruiting ship for plantation labour. Then there was a cable ship in twice a year, coming up from Australia and going on to Honolulu. And from time to time there were a number of American fishing vessels coming down from Hawaii.

I actually opened fire on one of these once, because it was inside the three-mile limit and they were pinching our fish. I thought, 'Well, I must attract their attention somehow.' I had a six-inch gun on the island, but this I daren't use because it was too dangerous. So I started firing a rifle ahead of them, but there was no response.

I duly reported the incident with a minute to government headquarters, saying this ship was within territorial waters and took no notice of my warning. I got a minute back about nine months later – that was the time it took to get the mail through from Tarawa – and it said, 'You really must not open fire on American fishing vessels.'

But when that particular fishing vessel came into Fanning

harbour the next time, the people on board were so nice, and after that they used to give us turkey and ice-cream from their stores, so we got to be very good friends.

On Christmas Island, Nicholson found himself faced with a new role in addition to his administrative duties. The manager of the government plantations became ill, and for the next six months Nicholson took his place, learning a lot in a short time about the cultivation of the coconut, including some of the legendary 103 names used for it by the islanders. He lived close to his Gilbertese labourers and shared a way of life that had its own strange rules and rituals.

For instance somebody buried a coconut shell with the opening upwards underneath the path where I would walk every day. He wanted to get a friend a job and he was making white magic to persuade me to take him on. Another thing was that people seemed to be affected by phases of the moon. I think when you're living on those islands, so far from anything or anyone, you feel nearer to the moon, the stars and the sea than you do to the earth, and the tides perhaps could affect you. Certainly we had one person I remember well. His family would come along just before full moon and say, 'Will you lock up our relative because he goes all funny at the full moon – he's apt to run around and be dangerous.' We'd help by shutting him up.

Some of the Europeans had their idiosyncrasies, too, in lonely places such as the Gilberts, but the longer they had lived there the less anyone was inclined to notice.

My first introduction to social life was a tea party given by the wife of the Acting Resident Commissioner who'd been there quite a time. It was a typical island house with a high thatched roof and no ceiling. Halfway through, my hostess suddenly said 'Excuse me!' and, rummaging in the cushions of the settee, brought out a small revolver. The next minute she fired it into the roof and a rat fell down dead on to the middle of the tea table. Some of the newcomers found it a bit startling, I remember.

The upheavals of the war had left little change in their wake in this part of the world. The stone bunkers built by the Japanese on Tarawa were soon covered by bush and vine, and the field gun on the lookout point, a trophy from Singapore, quickly rusted in the salty trade winds. The coral beaches were places of peace again and a District Officer such as Nicholson might imagine himself posted to Paradise.

You looked out on to what was two million square miles of sea. My office was on the lagoon side, and that was heaven. In those days, it was a thatched building with no walls, just blinds that dropped down for shade. I kept a swimming costume in my desk and in the afternoons when I'd finished, I'd get up, jump out on to the sand, then straight into the water.

Another post-war administrator in the Gilbert and Ellice Islands was Nigel Pusinelli, who arrived as Secretary to Government in 1946. A skilled yachtsman, he quickly established a rapport with the island boat-builders. One strange experience that followed seemed to belong to the Grimble era and showed how little the basic customs and beliefs of the Gilbertese had been affected by Western ways.

I was introduced to an old man called Tuami who said he would build a traditional racing canoe for me. But there was tremendous secrecy about it. A lot of magic was mixed up with how a canoe was built. He had two or three helpers, and I used to go and visit him every fortnight, take him food and see how the canoe was getting on. But nobody else was allowed in the hut where the canoe was being built.

After a couple of months it was virtually finished. At the same time the old man got sick and developed a huge swelling on his neck. So we took him up to the local hospital, and they said the only thing to do was to open it up. Tuami firmly refused any such suggestion, so the old man went back to his village, and there he lay for about three months and proceeded to die.

Immediately he was dead, the helpers who had been with him put the last plank on the canoe and a few weeks later it was brought down to me. It was called *Tekimatori*. It was the most splendid racing canoe and I had a wonderful time sailing in it.

Eventually one of the clerks in my office, who was related to the family, told me, 'Oh, Tuami broke a lot of the rules and customs in canoe-building. He thought he could really make a faster canoe than anyone else had ever done, and he recorded all this in a book. But there was so much magic in it that he felt this was his life's work, and that having done it, the only thing to do was to die. And so, you know, he just died. And as soon as he was dead, his wife burnt the book because she thought there was too much magic in it.

Pusinelli was also told that the old man had sinned against custom by building the canoe specifically for a European. On the other hand, because it was for a European, Tuami might have felt freer with it than if it had been for his own use. Certainly Pusinelli believed the old man had willed himself to die, whatever the reason. Such a canoe deserved to be preserved for posterity, and when the time came for Pusinelli to leave he gave it to his clerk, to keep in the family.

He sailed it himself and he used to take it out fishing. But the extraordinary thing was that, soon after, the boat capsized when he was out on the ocean beyond the reef. He was rescued, but the canoe drifted away. Everyone thought it was lost for ever, and then, weeks later, it was washed up on the exact piece of the beach where it had been built. So everyone said, 'Ah well, you know, *Tekimatori*'s come back to where it belongs, to Tuami.'

Traditional canoes were still used for getting from one island to another all over the South Pacific. Anne Sopper had to take whatever transport there was. Sometimes she was in a tightly packed barge, sat on by pigs and tickled by goats' tails. During one particularly disturbed journey she climbed up to the crow's nest to escape, and spent 'the best night I've ever had at sea', curled up on a coil of rope.

In Fiji she often made the river crossings by raft, a rudimentary craft of five poles of bamboo lashed together, with a large Fijian to do the punting. On the first of these crossings, just when they seemed to be sinking, he somewhat alarmed her by telling her that the raft was called HMS *No-Come-Back*. It was reassuring to find out later that this was the traditional nickname for these river rafts. The Fijians built them to take their bananas to market, and here they left them to drift or disintegrate, happy to walk home with their money in their pockets. Making new rafts for the next journey down was far less trouble than paddling the old ones back up-river, against the current.

Things could be even rougher in Tonga, especially if your destination was Tin Can Island, so called because the best way to get the mail ashore was simply to throw it overboard in a watertight container to be caught by the local postman who, not surprisingly, was the best swimmer on the island. Anne Sopper found herself despatched in the same way, caught in the arms of an immense Tongan waiting on an adjoining spit of rock. The alternative was to try to shoot the waves in an outrigger canoe, a miracle of timing which didn't always work. 'Instead of going in on the crest of the wave, we went in under it. We got out absolutely soaking, staggering up on to a beach of black volcanic sand, but the heat was so terrific that you dried in no time.'

The perils of getting ashore were of less concern to visiting Governors and High Commissioners. In most islands the traditional mode of transport had remained unchanged throughout the century. The all-important concern of the islanders was that at no point of the disembarkation procedure should the great man's feet touch ground, or rather water. And so His Excellency found himself borne aloft through waves on a sort of South Sea *howdah* – a bamboo platform surmounted by a chair or a boat, the whole edifice swathed with tropical flowers and foliage and carried on the broad shoulders of the welcoming party. When Sir John Gutch was visiting the Gilberts as late as 1960, as High Commissioner for the Western Pacific, the ceremonial was unchanged. Indeed, some of the islanders seemed to take a gleeful pleasure in harking back to the good old days.

As we got nearer the shore, I was seized on all sides and lifted on to a large canoe. The people had made a big fire on the beach and they carried me round this, shouting, 'Cook-im Kai-Kai! Cook-im Kai-Kai!' *Kai-Kai* is the word for food, and they were pretending that I was going to supply their next meal. But it was all good fun.

I remember another welcome we were given in the eastern Solomons. We were sitting around on the ground eating a rather indigestible feast and one old man got up and said he wanted to make a speech.

I said, 'Please do.'

And he said, 'Well, it's so nice to have you sitting with us, visiting us like this and eating our food. In the old days, sir, you would have also been at our feast, but most probably as one of the items on the menu.'

Everyone roared! This was the great joke of the day.

Even the reception for a Governor paled beside the great occasion of a royal visit. After the coronation of June 1953, newspaper and magazine pictures of the Queen and the Duke of Edinburgh were a favourite adornment of bamboo huts and village houses from Fiji to the New Hebrides, usually pinned to the central beam in a place of honour among the family photographs and the strings of white cowrie shells. Just six months later they were there in the flesh, making the famous tour that was to become a highwater mark in the long history of Anglo-Pacific relations.

Everywhere they went, the ceremonies of welcome were the most elaborate and colourful in living memory. The Governor's lady had to ensure that everything ran smoothly at the royal reception at Government House. As this was the South Seas, however, nothing went quite according to plan. The dinner party for eighty was a triumph, the long table glowing with decorations of tropical orchids and pineapples. Afterwards Lady Garvey escorted the Queen upstairs to powder her nose in a specially prepared retiring room, while she herself retreated into a small room alongside.

> I was in there, when suddenly a little voice called out, 'Lady Garvey, Lady Garvey!' Before I could move, the Queen rushed in. She said, 'There are two bats in the bedroom!'
> Well, of course, the only thing I couldn't control was bats. The windows were open and the bats had flown in. So I said, 'Well, what about using this mirror?' So she sat and powdered her nose until she was composed and ready to go downstairs again.

The Queen's tour of the Pacific was also the occasion for a reunion with a fellow monarch with whom a friendship had been formed at the time of the coronation. In 1953, Tonga's Queen Salote seemed destined to rule over her people until she reached a ripe old age. She was only as old as the century, and like Queen Victoria she had ascended the throne while still in her teens. Twelve years later, Queen Elizabeth appointed her first Dame Grand Cross of the Order of St Michael and St George to mark the longest reign in Tongan history. But national celebrations were marked by foreboding. Queen Salote was mortally ill and her public appearances grew rarer. Chronic diabetes had been succeeded by cancer and her strength was ebbing week by week.

But on one occasion it seemed to her that her presence was all-important. It was at a time when Tonga was anxious to benefit from the International Aid for Economic Development scheme. The construction of a deep-water harbour had been proposed with aid from Britain. But by international agreement the capital expenditure involved was dependent upon the workforce being covered by union protection. In the context of the Tongan way of life, the idea of trade unions was a revolutionary one. A special session of Parliament was convened, to be addressed by the Queen, and one of the guests at that session was Freda Gwilliam, who had come to know the Queen during her work for women's organisations in the Pacific.

The Queen was driven the hundred yards from the Palace to the Parliament building, and when she got out of the car she looked magnificent in a dress of deep cream satin, and around her waist the traditional frayed mat which is handed down from one generation to the next. This particular mat had been in her family for 300 years.

She had to carry a stick and this hurt her pride, but without it she would not have been able to walk up the hall. As she reached the steps, her eldest son, who was then Prime Minister, stepped out and quietly took the stick from her, so she mounted to the throne alone. Her ADC, who was her nephew, handed her her speech, and she stood there and began to talk to the assembled gathering of nobles and commoners. her opening words were, 'My dear old friends, times change and we have to change with them. But this is your decision and only you can make it.' At the end she came down the steps, her son handed her the stick, and with her head held high she walked out. It was the last time I saw her. Within a few weeks, she was dead.

The death of Queen Salote in December 1965 marked the end of an era, not in Tonga alone, but throughout the Pacific. As she had said, times were changing. Elsewhere the old colonial Empire was breaking up with an increasing momentum, often amidst scenes of recrimination and bloodshed. No such bitterness clouded the South Sea relationships, but it was evident to the administrators that the point had been reached for handing over their responsibilities.

Ever since the mid-1950s, it had been the official policy of government 'to prepare the people as rapidly as possible for advances in local government, as a basis for achieving a more advanced constitution'. The daring word 'independence' was not heard publicly until several years later. Apart from the more progressive politicians, in many of the islands nobody actually seemed to want the British to go. But go they must, even someone like Christine Woods, now matron of the Solomons' Central Hospital, who had been serving the Solomons for so long that the local people thought of her as a permanent institution. In 1973, to mark her forty years with the Melanesian mission, they decided to arrange a rather special celebration. For just a day, it seemed, 'Woodsie' too could be Queen of the Islands.

The priest in charge came to me and he said, 'Now look, Matron, this is no laughing matter. This is very serious. We haven't done this ceremony for a hundred years. You will wear *tapa* cloth tomorrow and no European clothes.'

I said, 'All right, I think it'll cover me.'

Then he told me the King would be there.

I said, 'You don't have kings in these islands.'

He said, 'For tomorrow we do.' In fact it was the paramount chief of Gela who was coming to pay a visit to his 'wife'.

So I said, 'And I am his wife?'

He said, 'Yes, you are. For the time being anyway.' I was also told that at no time at all was I to turn my back on the King. I was only to speak if he spoke to me. Then I was to have placed round my neck a ceremonial collar which hadn't seen the light for a hundred years, and adorning it were the longest and curliest pigs' tusks that could be found. Finally they were going to present me with this pig, and I was to give back two cases of corned beef and two cases of fish, for the feast. His last words were, 'Now remember, Matron, if you turn your back on the King, you'll get a spear in your back and that's serious.' It was the one thing I kept remembering all day, and it was quite a day.

Fifteen hundred Melanesians were there and nearly a hundred whites. It was a tremendous ceremony. Then, to end with, they did one dance which they could only do for a Queen. They did it later for Her Majesty when she came out, and they haven't done it since. That was their way of saying thank you to me.

There were things the British wanted to say thank you for, too. For all of them, the South Seas had become part of their lives, and whatever the future held, their years spent in the islands would somehow dominate almost every other experience. For Tom Russell there was one image that summed up all the rest.

You'd get way up into the hills that were covered in mist, and you'd go into a little house. In there you had a man, a woman, a child, fire, water, and food, the roof over their heads, and complete contentment. They had so little and so much. It always made me wonder what we Europeans had lost along the way, with our cars and our consumer society. I still remember that.

In these last years, the winds of change brought misgivings, too, as the British took stock of two centuries of Western influence on so vulnerable a part of the world. Guy Wallington, among others, remembers the kind of questions that were being asked.

> When you look back, what have these people had before? They've had missionaries converting them, blackbirders kidnapping them, ruffians and rogues, administrations and governments, all trying to impose on them something that's alien to them. Where has it all got them? Why can't they be left alone?

Now at last they were to be left alone, at least briefly, until the superpowers began to vie for their favours as they had done in the nineteenth century. This time, however, it would be for more serious prizes, such as harbours for nuclear vessels. Fiji led the way with independence in 1970, the same year that Tonga officially concluded its old-style relationship with Britain. The Solomons followed in 1978 along with the Ellice Islands, who reclaimed their traditional name of Tuvalu, and a year later the Gilberts emerged as the republic of Kiribati. The transformation was complete with the independence of the New Hebrides in 1980, to become the republican Vanuatu. All were to remain members of the Commonwealth.

For the British, who had experienced so many island embarkations, it was time to step aboard for the final journey, the one-way passage home. On Suva wharf, chief calling-point for the passenger liners, the sight of the Fiji Military Forces Band in their scarlet jackets playing the traditional song of farewell, *Isa Lei*, was guaranteed to bring a quiver to the stiffest of upper lips.

> Alas, indeed! I shall be so sad
> When you embark tomorrow.
> Please remember our happiness together.
> Keep on remembering the islands. . .

At the rail, someone was bound to tell you to throw your garland of frangipani into the white foam of the ship's wake. If it floated back to shore, it meant you would be coming back to the islands. But for most people, this was only a gesture. This time it really was goodbye.

Notes on Contributors

Andrew Armstrong, CMG Born 1907. Joined Colonial Administrative Service 1929, appointed to Western Pacific, Gilbert and Ellice Islands. Left 1940 for Nigeria.

Eric Bevington, CMG Born 1914. Joined Colonial Service as Administrative Officer, Gilbert and Ellice Islands 1937. District Officer, Fiji 1942, various subsequent posts there until 1962, including Assistant Colonial Secretary, Financial Secretary, Development Commissioner and Governor's Deputy.

John Brownlees Born 1910. Called to the Bar 1932, and appointed Administrative Officer, British Solomon Islands Protectorate 1933. Seconded to Kingdom of Tonga as Secretary to Government and Acting Chief Justice 1941–7. Appointed British Judge, New Hebrides, 1956–8.

James Coode, OBE Born 1918. Joined Colonial Service 1940 as District Officer, Gilbert and Ellice Islands. Administrative Officer, Fiji 1943–59, including two years' service as Clerk to Executive and Legislative Councils. British Commissioner and Consul, Kingdom of Tonga, until retirement in 1965.

Mrs Charis Coode Born 1919. Trained in Domestic Science. Posts as school matron, and war service in FANY and ATS, before marriage to James Coode 1947 and start of life in Pacific. Worked in Colonial Secretary's office, Suva.

The Hon Sir Alastair Forbes Born 1908. Called to the Bar 1932. Appointed Resident Magistrate, Fiji 1940. Solicitor-General, and Assistant Legal Advisor, Western Pacific High Commission.

Lady Constance (Irma) Forbes Daughter of Capt C. E. Hughes-White, RN. Married Alastair Forbes 1936.

Revd D. Lloyd Francis Born 1901. Work in Woolwich Dockyard, New Zealand dairy-farming and forestry, before joining Melanesian Mission 1926. Stationed various island groups in Solomons, including leper colony at Qaibaita. Later pioneer work in New Guinea and New Hebrides. Married Edith Piggot, Mission Hospital Nursing Sister, Fauaba 1934. Ordained Deacon, Solomon

Islands 1934, and priest in New Zealand. Pacific war service as Chaplain, New Zealand Armed Forces.

Sir Ronald Garvey, KCMG, KCVO, MBE Born 1903. Joined Colonial Administrative Service 1926 as cadet, attached to Western Pacific High Commission, Suva. District Officer Solomon Islands 1927–32. Assistant Secretary WPHC 1932–40. Acting Resident Commissioner, Gilbert and Ellice Islands Colony and New Hebrides Condominium. Governor and Commander-in-Chief Fiji 1952–8. Author of *Gentleman Pauper*.

Lady Patricia Garvey Born Fiji. Daughter of the late Dr V. W. T. McGusty, GMG, OBE. Married Ronald Garvey 1934.

John Goepel Born 1906. Joined Colonial Administrative Service 1928. Attached to Ratu Sir Lala Sukuna, paramount Chief, Fiji, to learn language and customs. District Commissioner various areas, took over 70 islands of Eastern District 1937. Left Pacific 1939. Author of Fijian language textbook.

Sir John Gutch, KCMG, OBE Born 1905. Entered Colonial Administrative Service 1928. Appointed High Commissioner for Western Pacific 1955. Retired 1961. Author of *Martyr of the Islands* and *Beyond the Reefs*.

Miss Freda Gwilliam, CBE Born 1907. Education Advisor to Colonial Office and Ministry of Overseas Development 1947–70. Many tours of the Pacific. Former Chairman, VSO Council, and former President, Women's Corona Society. Lifelong involvement with countrywomen's organisations throughout the world.

D. C. Horton, MA, DSC Born 1915. Overseas Civil Service 1936–57. Solomon Islands 1937–46. War service as Captain, Solomon Islands Defence Force and Lieutenant, RNUR (attached 1st US Marine Raider Battalion), awarded DSO, American Silver Star, and Conspicuous Gallantry Medal, State of Selangor, Malaya. Author of several books on Pacific including *The Happy Isles* and *Fire Over the Islands*.

Graham Leggatt Born New Zealand 1930. Teacher Suva Grammar School, Fiji 1950s, English Master Queen Victoria School 1960s. Appointed announcer, Fiji Broadcasting Commission 1955. Director of Broadcasting, Nauru 1968–71. Left Pacific for teaching posts in Middle East. Died New Zealand 1985.

R. A. Lever Trained in tropical agriculture. Went out to Solomon Islands 1931 to investigate coconut tree diseases affecting copra output. Transferred Fiji 1937 as entomologist. War service in Fiji Infantry Regiment. Posted to Malaya 1946. Contributor to journals on Pacific affairs.

Dr James (Jimmie) MacGregor, OBE Born 1927. Qualified St

Andrews University Medical School. Joined Colonial Medical Service 1951. Appointed to South Pacific Health Service in Solomon Islands 1956. Became Chief Medical Officer, subsequently Director of Medical Services. Retired from Overseas Service 1975.

Mrs Rita Moss MacGregor Born 1931. Trained and worked as physical education teacher until marriage to Dr Jimmie MacGregor 1955. Left Solomons 1975.

Kelvin Nicholson Left Navy to join Colonial Administrative Service 1946. Posted to Gilbert and Ellice Islands and served on Fanning Island, the Line Islands and Christmas Island in various posts, including District Officer, Wireless Operator, and Plantation Manager. At Tarawa 1951–5 as Cooperative Societies Officer, later broadcasting advisor and Secretary to Government. Transferred to Sierra Leone 1956.

Ronald Paine Born 1903. Appointed Assistant Entomologist Fiji Government 1925. Left Pacific 1934. Returned Fiji 1956 to work on biological control of crop pests. Appointment South Pacific Commission 1965–6.

Mrs Dora Patterson Born Fiji 1902. Descendant of early Fiji settler family. Has lived in Levuka since 1908. Husband Reg founded inter-island ferry service.

Mrs Sophia (Beausie) Pennington-Richards Born Nambavatu Island, Fiji 1915. Second daughter of Gus Hennings, plantation owner and descendant of William Hennings and royal family of Thakombau. Left Fiji 1936 to settle in England. Married 1951.

Nigel Pusinelli, CMG, MC Born 1919. Joined Colonial Service 1945. Served in Gilbert and Ellice Islands until 1957 as Secretary to Government, District Officer, District Commissioner, Cooperative Societies Officer, and Acting Resident Commissioner. Transferred to Aden 1958.

Bishop Derek Rawcliffe, OBE Born 1921. Ordained Worcester Cathedral 1945. Joined Melanesian Mission 1947. Assistant Master, All Hallows School, Pawa, Solomon Islands 1947, Headmaster 1953; St Mary's School, Guadalcanal 1956. Archdeacon New Hebrides 1958. First Bishop 1975. Resigned 1980.

Mrs Jane Roth Born 1910. Visited Fiji 1935 where uncle was Director of Medical Services. Married the late Kingsley Roth, former District Commissioner, Fiji, later Secretary for Fijian Affairs and author of *Fijian Way of Life*. Left Fiji 1958. Now keeper of the Fiji Collection, Cambridge Museum of Archaeology and Anthropology. Editor of Fijian journals of Baron Von Hugel.

The Ven R. C. Rudgard, OBE Born 1901. Went out as

missionary to Melanesia 1922. Schoolmaster until 1933. Principal of All Hallows School, Pawa, Solomon Islands. War service as Territorial Army Chaplain in Middle East. Died 1985.

Tom Russell, CMG, CBE Born 1920. Joined Colonial Administrative Service 1948 as District Commissioner, Solomon Islands. Assistant Secretary, Western Pacific High Commission, Fiji 1951. Deputy Commissioner, Solomon Islands 1954–6. Seconded Colonial Office. Financial Secretary 1965. Chief Secretary to WPHC 1970–74. Author of various monographs for Journal of Polynesian Society.

Dr Allenson Rutter Born 1912. Educated New Zealand and qualified Otago, London University and Royal College of Surgeons, Edinburgh. Appointed Medical Superintendent, Helena Goldie Hospital, Western Solomons 1938. Worked in Vella Lavella until Japanese invasion 1942. War service in British Defence Force as OC Medical Corps. Set up government hospitals and assisted various missions in medical work throughout the islands. Left Pacific 1948.

Mrs Elizabeth Rutter Born New Zealand 1915. Worked as microbiologist in hospital laboratory before marriage to Dr Allenson Rutter 1938. Assisted husband in medical work in Solomons. Lectured in UK for Central Office of Information and Commonwealth Institute on the south-west Pacific.

Miss Mavis Salt, MBE Born 1921. Trained in teaching and parish work London and Bristol. Teaching post with Melanesian Mission at Alanguala, Solomon Islands early 1950s. Appointed headmistress of girls' boarding-school, northern New Hebrides, also member of Government Education Committee. Retired to England after twenty years' service to education in the islands.

Mrs Rosemary Grimble Seligman Born on Tarawa atoll in Gilbert Islands, daughter of the late Sir Arthur Grimble, colonial administrator, writer and broadcaster. Artist and writer. Publications include *Migrations, Myth and Magic from the Gilbert Islands*, children's books, magazine articles, illustrations and photographs. Paintings and drawings exhibited at the Victoria and Albert Museum and elsewhere in London, Cyprus and Barbados.

Philip Snow, OBE, MA, JP Born 1915. Joined Colonial Service 1938. Provincial Commissioner, Magistrate and Assistant Colonial Secretary, Fiji and Western Pacific 1938–52. Founder Fiji Cricket Association 1946. Publications include *Cricket in the Fiji Islands*, *Best Stories of the South Seas*, *The People from the Horizon*, *Bibliography of Fiji, Tonga and Rotuma*, and numerous articles on the Pacific for journals and newspapers. Also author of *Stranger and Brother*, a portrait of his brother C. P. Snow.

Mrs Mary Anne Snow Born 1919. Went out to Fiji 1940 to marry Philip Snow in Suva Cathedral.

Miss Anne Sopper Posted to South Pacific early 1960s. As British Red Cross Regional Field Officer spent ten years touring the islands, including Fiji, Tonga, the Gilbert and Ellice, the Solomons and the New Hebrides. Left Pacific for Swaziland.

Sir David Trench, KCMG, MC, DL Born 1915. Appointed cadet Solomon Islands 1938. Seconded to Western Pacific High Commission 1941. War service as Lieutenant-Colonel Solomon Islands Defence Force 1942–6, MC, US Legion of Merit. Secretary to Government, Solomon Islands 1947. Left Pacific 1949, returning as High Commissioner Western Pacific 1961–3.

Sir Leonard Usher, KBE Born New Zealand 1907. Appointed teacher Fiji 1930, headmaster various schools. War service in Fiji Infantry Regiment. First head of government public relations. Editor *Fiji Times*, and has held numerous public offices. Retired and living in Suva.

Sir Alexander (Nick) Waddell, KCMG, DSC Born 1913. Joined Colonial Service 1937 and served in Solomon Islands as Cadet District Officer and District Commissioner until 1945. Pacific war service as Lieutenant RNVR 1942–4, Major Solomon Islands Defence Force 1944–5. Awarded DSC 1944. Left for appointments in Malaya, North Borneo, Gambia and Sierra Leone.

H. G. Wallington Born 1921. Joined Colonial Administrative Service 1949, appointed to Western Pacific High Commission. Solomon Islands 1950–58. New Hebrides Condominium 1958–77.

Quentin (Q) Weston Born 1918. Seconded from Army to Fiji 1940 as District Officer in Colonial Service. Later joined Fiji Military Forces and saw active service in Bougainville in the Solomons. Returned to District Administration in Fiji, apart from spell as HM Commissioner and Consul in Tonga, retiring in 1963 as Assistant Colonial Secretary. Appointed Chief Secretary to Republic of Nauru 1967, continuing as London representative until 1983.

Miss Christine Woods, OBE Trained as a nurse. Joined Melanesian Mission in Solomon Islands 1934. Appointed Matron main hospital 1951, started new hospital on island of Gela. Retired 1975. Solomon Islands Independent Medal 1977.

Keith Woodward, OBE Born 1930. Joined Colonial Service 1953 as Office Assistant, British Residency, New Hebrides Condominium. Administrative Service 1957–70, with special responsibility for District Affairs. Awarded Vanuatu Independence Medal 1970. Retired on medical grounds 1978.

Bibliography

Britton, J., *Fiji in 1870*. Melbourne, 1870.

Brown, J. Macmillan, *Peoples and Problems of the Pacific*. Fisher Unwin, 1927.

Campbell, Lord George, *Log Letters from the Challenger*. London, 1876.

Cargill, D., *Memoirs of Mrs Margaret Cargill*. London, 1855.

Cook, J., *Voyage to the Pacific Ocean in HMS the Resolution and the Discovery*. Dublin, 1784.

Cross, Gwen, *Aloha Solomons*. University of the South Pacific, 1982.

Derrick, R. A., *A History of Fiji*. Fiji, 1946.

Fiji Times (files of the newspaper). Suva, Fiji.

Garvey, Sir Ronald, *Gentleman Pauper*. Anchor, Bognor Regis, 1984.

Grimble, Arthur, *A Pattern of Islands*. John Murray, 1952 and Penguin, 1981.

Harrisson, Tom, *Savage Civilization*. Gollancz, 1937.

Horton, Dick, *Fire Over the Islands*. Reed NZ and Leo Cooper, 1970.

   The Happy Isles. Heinemann, 1966.

Lockerby, W., *Journal of a Sandalwood Trader*. Haklyut Society, 1925.

Markham, A. H., *The Cruise of the Rosario*. London, 1873.

Martin, J., *Mariners Tonga*. London, 1817.

Muspratt, Eric, *My South Sea Island*. Duckworth & Co. and Travel Book Club, 1931.

Neill, J. S., *Ten Years in Tonga*. Hutchinson, 1955.

Palmer, G., *Kidnapping in the South Seas*. Edinburgh, 1871.

St Johnston, T. R., *South Seas Reminiscences*. Fisher Unwin, 1922.

Snow, Philip, *Cricket in the Fiji Islands*. Whitcombe and Tombs, New Zealand, 1949.

Snow, Philip and Stephanie Waine, *The People from the Horizon*. Phaidon, Oxford, 1979.

Thomson, B., *Diversions of a Prime Minister*. London, 1894.

Williams, T. and J. Calvert, *Fiji and the Fijians*. London, 1860.